CONSTABLE
IN CONTROL

A perfect feel-good read from one of
Britain's best-loved authors

NICHOLAS RHEA

Constable Nick Mystery Book 14

JOFFE
BOOKS

Revised edition 2020
Joffe Books, London
www.joffebooks.com

Cover credit: Colin Williamson
www.colinwilliamsonprints.com

**Join our mailing list for free Kindle
books and new releases.**

www.joffebooks.com

We love to hear from our readers! Please email any
feedback you have to: feedback@joffebooks.com

ISBN 978-1-78931-595-0

CHAPTER I

Constable Nick was off duty and dressed in oily overalls. He was lying beneath his beautiful MG car which was safely jacked up while on the floor around him was a selection of his tools and a brand-new exhaust pipe, shining and clean. The dim light of his garage was barely sufficient to illuminate the scene but in the confined space, he was struggling to free a bolt somewhere beneath the car. That bolt had rusted so that it was difficult to move; it wasn't the correct type either, some previous owner having fixed the existing but worn-out old exhaust with the wrong-sized bolt. Unless it had become cross threaded? That was a possibility. Whatever the reason, the bolt was refusing to budge and it was stubbornly securing the burnt-out exhaust.

The exhaust pipe had developed a large hole which made it useless and illegal. Nick had partially removed it and it was now suspended, half on and half off, from the underside of the car, dangling like the broken branch of a tree. Unless it came completely off, he couldn't use, or even move, the car, nor could he complete the fitting of the new part.

And just one stubborn bolt held it! One small piece of metal was causing all this delay and frustration! He'd released all the others.

1

"There's always one!" he cursed to himself as he struggled to free the reluctant bolt. But it was immovable. He tried hammering it, hoping that this might dislodge it from its firm setting, or that blows from the hammer might loosen any rust which might be securing it. The snag was he couldn't get sufficient leverage — there was a bracket in the way and it was obstructing his efforts with the spanner. If he could remove that bracket, then he might be able to get more purchase on the head of the bolt by using a large adjustable spanner . . .

But before he could do that, he needed a bigger screwdriver to loosen that bracket! None of his was large enough . . . Nick sighed with frustration. This just wasn't his day! He'd hoped to complete this job tonight — now it would drag on until he managed to shift that stubborn bolt. If he didn't do something quickly, the car would be stuck here for days. And Aidensfield wasn't the sort of place where you could just pop out and buy a new screwdriver — that meant a trip into Ashfordly tomorrow. There'd be no shops open tonight.

Momentarily defeated, he eased himself from beneath the vehicle and was rising to his feet, rubbing his hands on an oily rag, when Kate came through from the house. She was casually dressed, also being off duty. Like Nick, she was hoping there'd be no call-outs this evening but, just like a policeman's duty, a doctor's work was never done.

"Problems?" she asked.

"Somebody's used the wrong bolt," he sighed. "It's either got rusted in or it's cross threaded. Whatever it is, I can't shift it so I can't get that exhaust off. I'll have to move a bracket to get better leverage and to do that I need a bigger screwdriver! And that's what I haven't got! I've got every size except the one I need!"

"Leave it for tonight, Nick, it's half past nine. Come on, it's time to put your feet up!"

At a moment of silence that followed, the sound of a speeding car could be heard outside. It was roaring past, hurtling along the street and making a tremendous din. It was evidently someone in a hurry.

"Somebody's in a rush! I wonder if it's an emergency?" said Nick throwing the oily rag to the floor. "I hope they're not coming here!"

"No, it's the third I've heard tonight," Kate told him. "It's probably a motor rally."

"A motor rally?" he cried. "I haven't been notified about any rally that's run through here, the police are supposed to be informed if motor clubs arrange rallies through any police area!"

"Forget it, Nick! You're off duty!" she emphasised. "And leave that rusty old bolt as well. Come along, you're tired. I'll get us something warm to drink and we can have an early night."

With a backward glance at the disabled exhaust pipe, he followed Kate out of the garage, switched off the light and somewhat reluctantly went into the house. He felt he'd been cheated of achieving his objective this evening, but Kate was right. He did feel tired and he was ready for a wash and a change of clothing. After all, the job could wait another day.

"I'll check at Ashfordly Police office in the morning," he said, partly to himself and partly to Kate as he strode into the lounge. "If there is a rally, there might be something in our files."

"Nick, forget it! You're off duty!"

But he was not allowed to forget the noisy cars. As he was sipping a welcome warm drink made by Kate, he could hear more vehicles roaring past at regular intervals. They were all heading in the same direction, all making for the moors beyond Aidensfield with lots of revving and the occasional screech of tyres.

"There *is* a rally!" he stressed. "Listen to them, tearing through the place. I'm going out for a look."

"Nick . . ." the tone of Kate's voice was enough to halt him, at least momentarily, and then the telephone rang. He hurried into his office to take the call, wondering whether it was for him or Kate. He snatched at the receiver.

"Aidensfield Police," he announced himself. "PC Rowan speaking."

"It's Adrian Fairbrother from Oxgang Cottage," the deep masculine voice was loud and well-spoken. "You really ought to do something about those noisy cars, Constable."

"Noisy cars, sir?" Nick pretended to be ignorant of the problem. Mr Fairbrother always found something to complain about and besides, he might be referring to some other vehicles.

"Coming through the village at one-minute intervals, they are," continued Mr Fairbrother. "Making one devil of a noise. One after the other, like a motor rally . . ."

"I've not been informed of any motor rallies tonight, sir," admitted Nick. "But I'll look into the problem."

"It shouldn't be allowed, disturbing the peace like that."

"I will definitely look into it, sir. Rest assured I'll do what I can, Mr Fairbrother. I'll keep you informed."

With a sound something like "Hrrumph", the caller replaced the telephone and Nick returned to the lounge of his home. "Not trouble, is it?" Kate asked. "A call-out?"

"It was old Mr Fairbrother complaining about noisy cars," he explained. "It makes a change from him complaining about noisy dances or noisy kids or noisy music or noisy doors being slammed at the pub! I'd better just pop out for a look, I might catch sight of a number plate or recognise one of the drivers. I can always stop one of the cars and warn the driver if it is someone local."

"You're not going out now, are you?" she asked. "You are off duty, remember!"

And at that moment, another roared past; this one added several loud toots on the horn as it passed the police house. Nick gritted his teeth and dashed to the window, but the car was out of sight. He managed to see the tail-lights disappearing into the darkness but was too late to see the number plate.

"They're asking for it . . . it sounds like locals to me, doing that . . . cheeky blighters! It's not some of the village lads, is it?"

"Nick, I thought we were going to have an early night? It is our day off, remember . . ."

He looked at her with mock seriousness.

"No, I have my duty to do; one's constabulary duty must be done . . ." and her face showed her disappointment and the beginnings of anger as he added, "So the last one into bed puts the light out!"

And he raced for the staircase.

* * *

For most of that same evening, the bar of the Aidensfield Arms had been almost deserted. George had expected one or two early customers but none had arrived. The only drinkers were a courting couple who had occupied one corner of the bar while sipping all night from just two drinks, and Claude Jeremiah Greengrass who had spread himself in front of the fire.

During the evening, the young lovers had been completely absorbed in one another. They had spent the entire time sitting close together over their drinks as they had gazed into one another's eyes and dreamt of future bliss. They hadn't shown the slightest bit of interest in chatting to George.

Claude, on the other hand, had had a half-consumed pint on a table at his side for ages and he'd been totally absorbed in an item in the pub's copy of the *Evening Gazette*. He had shown no desire to make small talk either. He'd spent a long time reading the paper, sipping from his pint as Alfred, his lurcher dog, had slept at his feet. Apart from the occasional words of endearment from the couple in the corner, no one had spoken; the only noise was the crackle of logs on the fire and the heavy breathing of the slumbering Alfred. He was probably dreaming about hectic pursuits of rabbits and pheasants.

5

George Ward, the licensee of the Aidensfield Arms, hadn't been able to remember when the bar had been so quiet at this stage of the evening, so he'd taken the opportunity to replenish his shelves from stock in the cellar. He'd carried several crates from below, puffing and panting as he'd staggered into the bar beneath their weight, and he'd then started to rearrange the bottles on shelves behind the bar counter.

"It's quiet tonight, isn't it, Claude?" George had commented as he'd taken a welcome breather from his labours.

Claude had not replied; his head had been deep within the pages of the paper. George had tried again, this time speaking in a louder voice.

"I said it's quiet tonight, isn't it, Claude?"

But on that second attempt at conversation, George had won another nil response. Claude had appeared not to hear him. So he'd tried again, this time using shock tactics and raising his voice by a few decibels.

"I said Adolf Hitler's bought that house behind the church, Claude."

That time, there had been a response.

"He'll have to do summat about that rising damp," Claude had muttered, not taking his eyes from the paper.

And so George had given up this attempt at being a friendly and chatty host. With customers like this, he could always amuse himself by fetching more bottles from the cellar or doing a crossword puzzle in the daily paper.

Having resigned himself to a long, boring evening, George had set about his self-imposed task, but when he had returned from that final trip to the cellar, Claude had gone. He'd vanished without even saying goodbye — he'd even vanished before closing time which made the event very unusual. And he'd taken Alfred with him. George had found it all very puzzling — Claude was usually so full of chatter. Furthermore, he was always on the scrounge, seeking free drinks or help with his dodgy business enterprises. But not tonight.

He'd been a different man! Tonight, he'd been totally absorbed in something he'd discovered in the newspaper.

And now George would never know what it was because Claude and his dog had disappeared without a word.

Pondering the situation, George went across to the table Claude had been using and began to clear it, but when he lifted the *Evening Gazette*, it fell open to reveal a large, ragged gap in one of the pages. Somebody had torn out an article . . . and that somebody must be none other than Claude Jeremiah Greengrass! It was just the sort of trick Claude would do . . . but what on earth had he torn out?

George re-folded the paper and placed it behind the counter so that he could read it after closing time, but the way things were going tonight, he could close early. And then, at the very moment he was savouring that thought, there were the familiar sounds of activity outside. Lots of cars were pulling up on the forecourt in rapid succession — suddenly, he was going to be busy! This was typical — a crowd of customers all arriving at the same time, and all expecting to be served! It would be a last-minute rush just before closing time!

The pub door crashed open and in came a horde of boisterous young people, youths and girls, all chattering noisily, laughing and joking as they made for the bar counter. Leading them was Gordon Turnbull. Tall, slim and good looking, Gordon was nineteen years old; rather arrogant in manner and smartly dressed, he worked for the family business of estate agents.

Never short of money, he always drove a smart sports car and always managed to be accompanied by a pretty young woman. From George's viewpoint, it always seemed to be a different girl — either Gordon was very fickle or else the girls he chose didn't find him permanently attractive. Tonight, he was followed in by Julie Mason, his latest conquest. She was a fine looking brunette whose splendid legs were shown to advantage by her mini-skirt. But Gordon was also accompanied by lots more youngsters, almost twenty of them by the look of it, and George recognised most. Many of them came from Aidensfield, Elsinby and the surrounding villages. They were an assortment of young people whose jobs ranged from farm labourers and garage mechanics to hotel receptionists and secretaries. All would be in their late teens, George reckoned.

"Right, George," began Gordon in his loud and commanding voice. "Drinks for everybody. And the slow worm's paying . . . tonight, that's him over there," and he pointed to a thin faced youth who was pushing his way forward to the bar. "Slim Jim Grieves."

"Slow worm?" puzzled George.

"Slowest around our club route, George. He did the slowest time tonight — you know, the Killing Pits Club. We do a circuit of Aidensfield, a drive around the moors, and the one who does the slowest time pays for drinks for everybody else. Great idea eh?"

"Bloody dangerous if you ask me!" George snapped. "I thought that club was for kids on bikes?"

"It used to be, George. When we were all kids on bikes, we called ourselves the Killing Pits Club because we met at the Killing Pits. We had races then, on our bikes. We had a slow worm then, kid's game I suppose, but we've kept it. When we were kids, the slow worm had to buy sweets for all the others. Anyway, now we've all grown up. The lads all got motorbikes with pillions to begin with, so we could take the girls out or go scrambling across the moors, and now we've all got cars. Same kids, same club, same rules, different transport."

"And you still meet at the Killing Pits?"

"Yes, we've been meeting there for years. We meet, have a chat about our cars and things, and now we've decided to do that circuit we did tonight. It's a bit of a challenge for us. And after doing the circuit, we'll come here for a few drinks. That's what we'll be doing at the Killing Pits Club meetings from now on."

"Well don't be surprised if there's complaints! If it's your cars that are making all that noise, you can bet somebody will start to make a fuss. You didn't do the run on your motorbikes, did you?"

"Not this run, George. We did moor scrambles then, away from public roads. But we need roads to drive our cars on."

"Well, I can guarantee there'll be trouble if you're racing through Aidensfield at night!"

"Racing? We're not racing, George, we go one by one, at one-minute intervals . . . that's a time trial, not a race!"

"It's a race so far as I'm concerned. Just watch it, Gordon, or you'll have PC Rowan on your backs! He'll say you're racing, he'll reckon a time trial is a race, Gordon, and don't forget — it could be dangerous, kids in old cars speeding like that . . ."

"Dangerous? Us? Come off it George! We're the best drivers for miles around. Besides, we'll make sure we do the run when Rowan's off duty. And we never drink before the run, that's a club rule. We celebrate afterwards. We're not daft . . . anyway, we're all here now so it's drinks all round on Slim Jim. So that's nine pints, three gin and tonics, two port and lemons, four Babychams — and something for yourself!"

As George began to pull the pints, he experienced a deep sense of foreboding and wondered if PC Rowan knew anything about the modernised Killing Pits Club.

CHAPTER II

Both Nick and Kate were on duty the following morning. Nick was scheduled to undertake a routine patrol of Aidensfield and district on his motorcycle. Sergeant Blaketon had instructed him to pay particular attention to detecting a spate of undetected thefts from church offertory boxes. The thefts had been occurring for a few weeks now with isolated rural churches being the main targets. The thief was creeping into the churches while they were not being used for services, breaking into the wooden offertory boxes and taking the contents. A considerable amount of cash had been stolen, albeit in individual small sums, and Sergeant Blaketon was determined to have the thief arrested.

With that task to occupy Nick, Kate was faced with a morning surgery in her temporary premises at the village hall, followed by a visit to Ashfordly Nursing Home. Afterwards, she had her rounds to complete. It looked like being a busy day for both.

Nick was first out of bed. He had washed and shaved and was preparing breakfast while Kate had her morning bath. Clad in his uniform trousers and a shirt without a tie, he had prepared a hefty meal of fried eggs, sausages, bacon and mushrooms. It was all sizzling on the stove and the smell gave him a hearty appetite.

He was looking forward to the meal when the telephone rang. Leaving the savoury offering, he went into the office to take the call.

"Aidensfield Police, PC Rowan," he announced himself.

"I wish to register my annoyance at that motor rally last night," said the haughty voice of Mrs Bridget Maitland. "Dozens of cars hurtling through the village, Constable, and all that noise and revving . . . you will take the appropriate action to end the nuisance, won't you, PC Rowan?"

"Yes, of course, Mrs Maitland," sympathised Nick. "I am going to Ashfordly this morning and I will check our records to see who the organisers were, then we shall contact them to express our deep concern about the disturbance that was caused. Rest assured we shall take very positive action to prevent a recurrence."

"I should think so too! These people really are the limit," she went on. "Using our lanes for their doubtful pleasures, making all that noise and pollution. I really think motor rallies ought to be banned and I'm surprised the police allow them. There is absolutely no need for them, they do not fulfil any useful purpose and I shall write to my Member of Parliament about it! I will demand that he takes action to have these silly rallies banned . . ."

"Yes, well, I will make sure the organisers are aware of our concern . . ." he tried to interrupt her non-stop verbal flow but he failed.

She went on and on about rallies and motor cars, about pollution of the air with their fumes and invasion of one's living space with their noise, not to mention damage to roadside verges, railings and fences, coupled with injuries to wild animals and moorland sheep.

As she ploughed on with her complaint, Nick smelt smoke.

"Mrs Maitland . . . I must go, there's a fire . . . smoke . . ."

"Yes, well, so long as you do something, Constable. If not, I shall feel obliged to write to your chief constable and another thing, I really ought to mention the mud that some farmers are leaving on the roads."

"Goodbye, Mrs Maitland and thanks for calling!"

He slammed down the handset and ran into the kitchen where his frying pan was fiercely ablaze. His attempt at making breakfast was doomed, for all he had produced was a pile of blackened ashes which were stuck to the frying pan. He whipped the pan off the heat and was wise enough not to place it under the tap; the effect of cold water on hot fat would be disastrous and dangerous, so he found an old floor cloth, soaked it in water and spread it across the pan.

It smothered the flames even if it did produce a lot of smell and smoke, but a quick examination of the bonfire told him the pan was ruined. It would require something with the power of a road drill to shift that mess! He placed the pan on the draining board to cool off and would dump it in the dustbin when he'd finished eating.

Now, he'd have to settle for a breakfast of toast and marmalade. He made enough for Kate and was sitting down to his own meal when she burst in.

"You never said it was so late!" she cried. "I was really enjoying a soak and thought it was eight o'clock but it's nearly nine o'clock and it's surgery . . . where's my diary, my prescription notes . . . Nick? Keys? Where's my car keys . . . ? I'm late and you know what people are like if they have to wait for the doctor . . ."

"Calm down, love, a couple of minutes wait won't hurt anybody!"

Kate ignored him and continued to dash around the house grabbing her coat, her brief case and other belongings before she halted and sniffed the air.

"Nick? Something's burning? What is it? Can't you smell it?"

"It's nothing to worry about now, love. It's finished, somebody rang about those noisy cars when I had the pan on but I've put it out."

"Put it out? Put what out?"

"The fire in the frying pan. It was those sausages. I had no idea sausages could do that, spontaneous combustion I think it must have been!"

She went across to inspect the ghastly mess in the remains of the flying pan, a wedding present.

"Nick, the pan is ruined! You could have burnt the house down, you really should be more careful."

"It was Mrs Maitland nattering, she went on a bit . . ."

"Look, I haven't time for anything," she had resumed her frantic activity while trying to put on her coat. "I haven't time for any breakfast and haven't time to stay and talk. I must open surgery in two minutes then afterwards I'm going to Ashfordly, to the nursing home. And while I'm there, I thought I would put some flowers on my grandparents' grave in Ashfordly churchyard."

"Then you'll have time to get a new frying pan while you're there?" he grinned mischievously.

She was now heading for the door, with one arm still not in the correct sleeve of her coat. She was desperately trying to find the right place for her hand.

"Yes, all right."

"So you'll be going to the ironmongers?" he persisted, delaying her even longer.

"Yes, of course. Look, I must go." Now she had found the right armhole and managed to thrust her arm down the sleeve. She was heading for the door now, a picture of bustle and haste.

"Then you can get me a screwdriver at the same time, so I can get that exhaust pipe finished."

"Screwdriver?" she cried. "I thought you were going to Ashfordly as well, to check on motor rallies or something. You can get your own screwdriver — and a new frying pan! It was you who ruined the one we've got!"

"I'm not supposed to go shopping when I'm in uniform," he smiled in his most charming way. "You know what Sergeant Blaketon's like about that sort of thing. Rules are rules — no private shopping while in uniform . . ."

"All right, all right, I'll get your screwdriver . . ."

"A large one, three-eighths blade," he said. "That's very important!"

"Right! Now get that smelly frying pan out of the house, will you? It's awful . . . it's like somebody burning horse manure!"

"Yes, love," he beamed.

"Why do I get myself talked into these things?" demanded Kate as she finally left the house, banging the door behind her.

"It's because you love me!" Nick shouted as she departed.

He returned to the business of the ruined frying pan and just as he collected it from the draining board, the telephone rang. Sighing, he went to answer it, still carrying the pan like a tennis racket. It was someone else complaining about noisy cars last night and this time, the caller thought the Monte Carlo rally must have been routed through Aidensfield.

Nick assured the gentleman that it was not the Monte Carlo rally; he'd have known if that event had been scheduled to pass through the village! He added that he would do all within his power to trace the organisers of last night's event so that due representations could be made. The caller appeared to be satisfied, and so Nick went outside, threw the blackened flying pan into the dustbin and returned to the kitchen to wash the pots. Only then could he prepare for his own tour of duty.

* * *

As Nick and Kate were beginning their day in Aidensfield, Mrs Joan Forrester and her son Graham were preparing for a weekend away from home.

Joan, recently widowed, was the former wife of Sergeant Blaketon. She'd divorced the sergeant, re-married but had recently lost her new husband. Sergeant Blaketon was the officer in charge of Ashfordly Police Station, and Graham was their son. Now aged eighteen, Graham was in his final year at secondary school and still pondering his future. But a weekend away sounded a good idea; he'd been invited to stay with his long-time friend, Denis Myers. Denis lived at Aidensfield with his parents. As small children at primary school, the boys had been inseparable and had always kept in touch, even as young men.

Joan Blaketon, on the other hand, had initially found life as a divorcee quite tough; her social life had almost ceased and she'd found it difficult to make new friends.

She had tried to make a success of her marriage to Oscar Blaketon but had decided, with reluctance, that he was more in love with his job than with her. And so they had divorced some years ago, with Joan getting custody of their son. She'd moved to Pickering where she'd found work, and then she'd met and married Alan Forrester who worked in a printing office. But Alan had died prematurely less than a year ago and now she was alone, with only Graham for company. From time to time, she did meet her former husband and their relationship was fairly amicable.

Looking forward to her weekend break, she'd done the washing and ironing and now, as she packed her case, she saw that Graham was outside, washing the car. He was keen to go for his weekend break too and she smiled at his ploy — he'd just passed his driving test and his new enthusiasm for cleaning the car was his way of softening her so she might allow him to drive to Aidensfield! She allowed him to work without interruption.

Having finished her own preparations, Joan went outside to see how Graham was progressing. He had washed the vehicle with a brush and hose and was now drying it with a wash leather, polishing the chrome and glass and standing back from time to time to admire his handiwork.

"You have done a good job!" beamed Joan, her dark eyes showing her pride. She was a handsome woman, tall and slender with a head of thick dark hair and warm eyes.

In many ways, Graham resembled her because he was tall and slender. His dad, she often thought, was of a more stocky nature, heavier and not so agile — all very good for the stolid image of a rural policeman!

"Well," beamed Graham. "We can't have you going off to Whitby in a scruffy old car, you never know who you might bump into!"

"I'm only staying with my friend Margaret and we're off to the Spa Theatre to see a play, just the two of us! There's no blind dates or anything like that, I'm not looking for romance, Graham!"

"Will you be seeing Dad?" Graham asked.

"I haven't any plans to see him, we are divorced remember! But look, it's his birthday on Sunday and I think you ought to get him a card and a present. I'm just popping down to the paper shop now, to tell them I'll be away for the weekend. I'm getting a card to post to your dad, so shall I get one for you to send?"

"Thanks, Mum, yes I'd like that. And I'll get him a present while I'm away — I can take it to him. Any idea what he'd like?"

"To be honest no, not at the moment. I'll think about it as we're driving over the moors. Now we'll set off in, say, an hour from now, shall we? We can get some lunch on the way, stop at a moorland pub perhaps. You're all packed, are you?"

"Just about. But relax, I'll be ready on time, Mum!"

"And I expect you'd like to drive, wouldn't you?"

His eyes lit up with excitement.

"Can I really? Your car? All the way to Aidensfield?"

"You've passed your test so that means you're capable, doesn't it?" she smiled. "So it's a deal — you drive and I'll make sure I'm not a backseat driver!"

* * *

Meanwhile in Aidensfield, Graham's friend, Denis Myers, was worrying about a peculiar rash which had appeared on his arms. He'd tried to ignore it, thinking it might go away, but when his mother saw it, she told him to get straight down to the surgery.

"You never know what you might have picked up, our Denis!" She always called him "our Denis" and some of his pals copied her. "Working on them building sites like you do, you could have got anything. So get yourself down to the village and see Dr Rowan. I just hope it's not catching! And don't forget you've got Graham Blaketon coming to stay tonight — we don't want him infected with whatever it is, so if the doctor says it's infectious, you'll have to ring Graham and tell him not to come. Now, surgery's open till ten o'clock and there'll be a queue, there always is, so you'd better be off."

Denis went to the garage behind the house, opened it and began to manoeuvre his motorcycle into the yard. It was a small machine, a BSA Bantam, one he'd had since he was sixteen.

Parked beside it was his dad's Austin A40 but Denis had not passed his test for motor cars, so he wasn't allowed to take out the car. His mum couldn't drive which meant she could not accompany him or give him lessons. On top of that, his dad was away a lot at sea, so poor Denis had very few opportunities to drive the car or to learn how to drive. Worse still, most of his mates now had cars of their own — old bangers most of them, but they were roadworthy and they helped enormously when it came to attracting girls. Denis sighed. All his mates had money and girls, he had neither. One day though, when he had saved enough money, he'd buy a car of his own. It would be a sports model with a red body and wire wheels . . . one day . . .

He kicked his motorbike into life, settled upon the saddle and rode down to Dr Rowan's surgery. The surgery was currently being held in a room at the village hall because when Dr Ferrenby died, his relatives had sold the house in which the surgery was contained. This had left young Dr Rowan without any suitable premises; for a time, she'd used a room in the police house but the village hall committee had allowed her to use one of the smaller rooms as a temporary measure. And so it was to the village hall that Denis drove, passing one or two other patients who were walking the same way.

Denis awaited his turn with patience and was finally admitted to the doctor. She smiled and asked him to be seated, then asked about his problem. He told her about the rash on his arms, explaining how it had arrived so quickly.

The doctor made a swift examination then asked about his work — he was an apprentice bricklayer — and what he and his mum kept at home, such as pets or flowers, or what kind of food he ate.

"Well," she said after a while. "It's an allergy, Denis. I'm not sure what you are allergic to, but it could be something you're in contact with at work like brick dust or cement powder, or it might be something in your home, like the cat, or certain flowers, food even. Different people can be allergic to different things."

"Is it serious? Is it catching?" there was some worry in his face.

"No, it's not serious and it's not infectious. You won't pass it to anyone else, so you can relax. Now, the only way to find out what's causing it is to be aware of everything you touch or come into contact with . . . it might take a long time to work out what's causing the rash — and once you've done that, then you keep away from whatever it is! For example, if the rash has just broken out, it could be caused by some new product at work — so keep your eyes and ears open and try to find out what it is!"

"But you can cure it, can you? It itches like mad, makes me scratch all night, in bed . . ."

"I'll prescribe some tablets for you," and she went across to her medicine cabinet and took a bottle of tablets from the shelf.

"These are called antihistamine tablets, Denis," she continued. "Start taking them tonight, when you go to bed. Have one at bedtime, one before breakfast and another one in the middle of the day, around lunch time or dinner time as you call it. Do that for a week, and the rash should clear up. Do you understand that?"

"Yes, sure, thanks," he rolled down his sleeves and waited as she wrote the instructions on the label.

But before handing him the tablets, she looked at him steadily and said, "Now this is important, Denis, so listen carefully. Once you have taken the first tablet, you must not drive — no driving cars or motorbikes. These tablets will make you feel dizzy — and on top of that, there's no drinking alcohol either. Now that's very important. It's only for a week or so, so it's not exactly a prison sentence! I want you to understand that, it is extremely important."

"Yes, sure, doctor. Right, thanks. It'll be worth it to get rid of this itching! I can get a lift to work, so I won't need to ride my motorbike."

"No, I'm going to sign you off work as well, that's during the time you'll be taking the tablets. We can't have you getting dizzy if you're working on scaffolding or while you're building walls, can we? So, it's eight days off work, starting from now. And come and see me in a week's time."

He indicated his understanding as she signed the necessary certificate, but as Denis Myers left the surgery, she felt uncertain as to how carefully he would obey her instructions.

She decided to keep an eye on Denis Myers over the next few days.

CHAPTER III

That same morning, Claude Jeremiah Greengrass was preparing for his exciting day's work while Sergeant Blaketon was beginning his duty at Ashfordly Police Station.

Claude, with the faithful Alfred at his side, left his tumbledown home in a very happy state; the day held a lot of promise because it had presented an opportunity to earn a large and very useful sum of money. On this occasion, it was a lawful sum of money, although Claude had decided that the tax man might never know about it.

For Sergeant Blaketon, on the other hand, the new day held the rather bleak prospect of an unannounced visit from the new inspector. She might arrive at any time of the day or night. She'd be coming to find fault with Ashfordly section, she'd be coming to check all the station registers and records, to see if the men had smart haircuts, polished boots and pressed uniform trousers, to check on the number of arrests and prosecutions and to see how the crime detection rate was progressing.

The lady in question was the formidable Inspector Murchison who was now based at Whitby. Due to recent divisional boundary changes, Ashfordly, Aidensfield and the surrounding villages lay in Whitby sub-division, of which she was the officer in charge.

Somewhat apprehensive about her propensity for making unannounced supervisory visits, Sergeant Blaketon was in his office very early that morning. He was checking every possible thing that might attract the critical attention of Inspector Murchison because she had a reputation for being meticulous in her scrutiny of the police stations she visited. To prepare for her, he even dusted the mantelshelf, swept up some coal dust from the hearth and placed new toilet rolls in the cells. One's prisoners must have every consideration; constables, on the other hand, had to bring their own loo rolls!

Then the telephone rang. He answered it.

"Sergeant Blaketon, officer in charge, Ashfordly Police," he identified himself.

"Inspector Murchison speaking, Sergeant," responded the deep and familiar voice. "I hope I've not got you out of bed?"

"Bed, ma'am? I've been at work for hours, this is a very busy section, you know. There's no slacking here! We are highly regarded by the public and highly efficient, renowned for giving a first-class service to the public."

"I like my officers to be good timekeepers, Sergeant, as well as being dedicated to their work and never afraid of doing their duty. Now, down to business, I require one sergeant and two constables for football duties. In Whitby tomorrow afternoon. A cup tie."

"From Ashfordly, ma'am? But I can't spare that number of men at such short notice. We're in the middle of a crime wave here and there's patrol duties, the office to manage."

"Ah, the crime wave! The offertory box thefts. You've not caught the thief yet, I note. Dozens of churches have been raided and several hundred pounds stolen over the past weeks and yet there's not a single arrest! It's not good enough, Sergeant Blaketon. I'd have thought it was simple enough for you to lay a trap and catch the thief or thieves."

"Rest assured we are concentrating upon that series of crimes, ma'am, my men are visiting all churches on a regular basis, liaising with the resident priest or vicar, checking the offertory boxes, showing a uniformed presence in vulnerable areas and acting as deterrents . . ."

"Yes, well, I look forward to an arrest very soon. It would greatly help your "crimes detected" figures. Now to the reason for my call. You will supply one sergeant and two constables at Whitby football ground tomorrow at two o'clock in the afternoon, dressed in their best uniforms. Kick-offs at three. I will brief your team when you arrive."

"Me, ma'am? You want me to come?" There was a hint of horror in his voice. Oscar Blaketon was the officer in charge of Ashfordly section, not a mere town patrolling sergeant with football matches to worry about.

"You are the sergeant at Ashfordly, aren't you? Now, this is a cup match, Sergeant, a quarter final, Whitby Town versus Crook. A big crowd's expected. I want no bus loads of fans fighting on our streets or in the ground. Is that understood?"

"Fans fighting? There'll be no fighting while my men are on duty, ma'am, you'll get the cream of Ashfordly section, men capable of the utmost diplomacy, men who can control the very worst of situations . . ."

But she'd rung off. He was talking to himself. He slammed down the handset and stalked along the passage to the general office. And there, seated in a cloud of cigarette smoke, was PC Alf Ventress. He was reading a newspaper but upon hearing Blaketon's office door being opened, he was able to hide it beneath his desk.

"Ventress!" snapped Sergeant Blaketon. "That woman has no idea how to run a police force! What's more important, do you think? Solving crime or playing football?"

"I'm not with you, serge!"

"We're in the middle of a serious crime wave and she wants us to perform duty at Whitby tomorrow!"

"It'll be nice at the seaside, serge," smiled Ventress.

"Nice? It won't be nice where we're going. It's football duties, Ventress, keeping fans from kicking each other's heads in."

"You'll see the match, though, from the touchline. That's a bonus, free entry to the game. So who's going, serge?"

"Me, as officer in charge of the Ashfordly contingent," and his chest expanded with pride at his own description, "I'm taking PCs Rowan and Bellamy."

"Bellamy can't go, serge," beamed Ventress. "He applied for the day off tomorrow. Remember? You approved it."

"Did I? Why's he want the day off?"

"He's playing football, serge, for Whitby Town."

"Football? Has the world gone mad, Ventress! There are times I think the police force is obsessed with sport, some people obviously think it's more important than real police work. Well, if he's not available, Ventress, you'll have to go."

"Me? But who'll look after the office?"

"We'll close the office, Ventress. The public will have to manage without us. The way things are going in the police service, we'll be closing offices all over the place because people want to watch or play football. That's progress, Ventress, progress towards a crime-ridden and undisciplined society. Take my word, it's the start of the destruction of our society, Ventress, but orders are orders. So it's best uniform tomorrow — brushed free of cigarette ash before you leave and kept free of cigarette ash while you're there! Leave your filthy fags at home, Ventress, then you won't be tempted. Now, where's Rowan?"

"He's on his way into the office, serge, with a careless driving file."

"Right, I'll brief him when he arrives. Now, if that woman rings, tell her I'm out."

"Where shall I say you are, serge?"

"Say I'm out patrolling the town, Ventress, doing what I'm supposed to be doing. Preventing crime, solving crime, being a policeman, doing what I'm paid to do! Not playing football, not watching football, not discussing football and not even worrying about rampaging football fans . . ."

And he stomped into his office and slammed the door.

* * *

Nick, en route to Ashfordly with the completed careless driving file in the pannier of his motorcycle, was approaching the Killing Pits junction of Aidensfield when he noticed the distinctive khaki clad figure of Claude Jeremiah Greengrass. Claude, with Alfred trotting behind on a long lead, had parked his old pickup truck outside the parish church and was ambling towards the gate which led into the churchyard.

Driving slowly, Nick watched the big man; Claude was carrying a scythe over his shoulder and in one hand he held a strickle, the North Riding of Yorkshire name for the whetstone used for sharpening the scythe. The strickle dangled from a leather loop; the implement was about fifteen inches long and shaped rather like a plumpish stick! With these implements in his hand, and with Alfred on a long lead, Claude approached the turnstile. His bulk and his encumbrances made it almost impossible to negotiate it.

The handles of the scythe got caught in the frame of the gate; Claude's bulk meant he had to lift the scythe high to clear the top of the gate, and then the strickle hit him in the face . . . but after much cursing, panting and puffing, he squeezed through. During all these manoeuvrings, however, Alfred remained outside the gate, on the end of the lead.

"Come on, Alfred!" shouted Claude. But the dog either would not or could not negotiate this gate. After all, these gates were especially designed to admit humans while frustrating animals like cows, horses and the free-range moorland sheep which roamed the village green. Claude tugged on the lead, shouted at Alfred, cursed him and tried to compel him to enter the turnstile, but Alfred steadfastly refused. Nick stopped his ride to observe the fiasco, whereupon Claude decided he must retrace his steps to deal with his dog.

And so the charade resumed, this time with Claude trying to get out of the churchyard; he hadn't the sense to leave his scythe and strickle inside, nor to release the lead, and thus began another elephantine ballet as Claude coped with the turnstile. When he was back in the street, he shook a finger at Alfred.

"All you have to do, you daft bugger, is walk through that gap, you bend your body in the middle . . . like I do . . . now come on!"

And as Claude made a further attempt with scythe, strickle and dog, Nick decided to drive closer.

He chugged along to the church and parked his motorbike near the gate, leaving it as he approached the struggling, cursing Claude.

"Are you trying to get in or out, Claude?" he grinned.

"Interfering coppers . . . ought to mind their own business . . . there's no peace from the law these days . . ." muttered the embattled Claude. By now, he was back inside the churchyard, but Alfred was still outside on the end of his lead.

"Drop your end, Claude," suggested Nick.

"Don't be personal, Constable!" retorted Claude.

"The lead, drop your end of the lead," repeated Nick.

"That's typical of the law, arresting a defenceless dog for loitering."

"Don't be daft, Claude, I'm going to get him into the churchyard!"

"You incomers think you know everything!" and Claude dropped his end of the lead and stood to watch Nick, beaming in anticipation of Nick's futile attempt. Nick withdrew the lead through the gate, went to the other large gate a matter of a few feet away, opened it and said, "Shout for Alfred, Claude!"

"That un's always locked!" snapped Claude. "It's only used for funerals and weddings!"

"Not today it isn't," grinned Nick, opening the gate wide. "See, no problem! It opens easily!"

"Well, how was I to know that? You just stood there and let me look stupid! Alfred, come here, you daft bat!"

Tail wagging, the scruffy grey dog trotted towards his master and obediently sat at his feet.

"So there we are, Claude," Nick had closed the gate and was now facing Claude who blinked at him and tried to avoid the gaze. "One good turn deserves another. So what are you doing here?"

"Cutting grass, aren't I?"

"But this churchyard's always neatly cut."

"Not under them trees, it isn't!" grinned Claude, pointing to a distant corner beneath some yews.

"And what do you charge for your services?" asked Nick.

"Nowt! I'm charging nowt. I'm a pillar of this community, Constable, and I'm doing my social duty to this village and others. Free gratis. For nowt. No pay or expenses."

"Really?" Nick wasn't quite sure how to take this news.

"You don't believe me, do you? It's a sod when a well-respected citizen like me can't do my social duty without the law suspecting him of summat."

"And you're using that old scythe? I thought you'd need something more modern!"

"I can't afford a new scythe, besides this un's just right for them awkward spots near tombstones, far better than them motor mowers."

"So you're doing other churchyards?"

"Glutton for work, I am, when I'm doing it for a good cause."

"The good cause being you, eh? So, Claude, have you seen any other suspicious characters hanging about the churches?"

"Other?" there was a tone of hurtfulness in Claude's voice.

"Somebody's going round raiding offertory boxes. Smashing them open with a screwdriver or jemmy and stealing the cash."

"It's your job to find 'em, Constable, not mine! Why should I help you, tell me that?"

"Because you are a pillar of the community, a well-respected citizen."

"Aye, well, I've seen nowt and I know nowt, but if I do see summat, I'll let you know. I can't be fairer than that, I reckon nowt to folk who rob churches. Now, I've the Lord's work to do, not the constabulary's!"

And as Claude ambled away towards the overgrown portion of the churchyard with Alfred following off the lead, Nick watched him for a few moments. He was sure Claude was involved in some dubious scheme; those blinking eyes, his avoidance of eye contact and the mere fact he was here indicated some scheme of a dodgy nature. It was hardly likely that Claude was simply cutting grass out of the goodness of his heart. Nick decided to keep an eye on him, but in the meantime decided to enter the church to check the offertory box. Happily, it was secure. No attempt had been made to break it open or steal the contents. He made a note in his pocket book of the date and time he'd made this check, then decided to resume his journey to Ashfordly.

But when he emerged from the turnstile, Alfred was sitting outside, looking forlorn and wanting to be in.

"How did you get out here, old son?" grinned Nick and as he opened the larger gate once more, he heard Claude shouting, "Alfred, you mutt, where the hell are you?"

Alfred trotted into the churchyard once again to be reunited with Claude as Nick kicked his motorcycle into life and rode off to Ashfordly. When he arrived at the police station with the careless driving file in his hands, Alf Ventress was seated among his usual cloud of smoke and Phil Bellamy was entering some details into a register. Bidding them good morning, Nick dropped the file into the "In" tray for Sergeant Blaketon's attention as Alf asked, "Hello, Nick. I've some good news for you and some bad news. Which do you want first?"

"Try me with the good news!"

"You're on football duties tomorrow at Whitby!"

"Great," beamed Nick. "That means I'll see the match. So what's the bad news?"

"Blaketon's going with you!" chuckled Bellamy turning from his work.

"Look, don't speak so loud, he's in his office," Ventress warned them. "Now look, while you're both here, listen to this. It's his birthday tomorrow. Seeing he's divorced and has nobody to celebrate it with, how about us all clubbing together to get him a present and a card? Something from the lads?"

Nick and Bellamy were both delighted with the idea and gave their agreement, with Bellamy saying he was on patrol duties in the town, so he could buy something. He'd pay for the gift and the others could settle up with him later. And the moment they had organised that little surprise, the sergeant's office door opened and out strode Sergeant Blaketon. He looked fiercer than usual.

"I might have known," were his first words. "Smoke and ash everywhere, my men gossiping and not doing any work! Nothing changes in this establishment. I dread to think what the new inspector would think if she walked in now! There's work to do out there, all of you, information to gather, traffic to control, crimes to solve, thieves to arrest . . ."

"Good morning, Sergeant," smiled Nick. "Nice morning!"

"Has Ventress briefed you about tomorrow's duties, Rowan?"

"Yes, Sergeant."

"Good, then I'll pick you up at Aidensfield Police House at one o'clock tomorrow. Prompt. Best uniform, boots polished, trousers pressed. The Ashfordly contingent will be the smartest men there, Rowan. And that means you, Ventress!"

"Yes, Sergeant," muttered Alf.

"Very good, Sergeant," said Nick and he turned to Phil Bellamy. "Aren't you going, Phil?"

Sergeant Blaketon answered for Bellamy.

"He is not gracing us with his presence, Rowan, because he's the star player for Whitby Town. Centre forward no less. He's far too busy to be a policeman, he's a footballer, Rowan," and Sergeant Blaketon turned to Bellamy. "And mind you score, Bellamy! If you don't I'll put you on permanent nights!"

"I'll score, serge, either with my feet or with a woman!"

"Right! That's settled. Now there's another matter," continued Sergeant Blaketon. "On Sunday, I shall be taking a day's leave. That means you will be in charge during my absence, Ventress."

"Something special, serge?" Ventress wondered if Blaketon was having some kind of birthday treat.

"I'm going for a spot of culture, Ventress."

"Not the Palace of Varieties at Scarborough, serge?" chuckled Bellamy.

"That's the sort of crack I'd expect from somebody who puts football before police work! No, I'm going to the Parsonage at Haworth, a literary trip with the Bronte Society."

"Well, have a nice day, serge, we'll just have to struggle along without you!" smiled Bellamy.

"And when I get back, I shall expect you to have arrested the offertory box thief, one or other of you. Now, the latest information is that a motorcycle has been heard at the raided churches, and its presence coincides with the time of the attacks. Also, the tool used to break open the boxes has been identified as a screwdriver with a three-eighths blade.

"A good impression was found at one church, the CID has taken a plaster cast for future comparison. That's enough clues for Sherlock Holmes, so it should be good enough for you. So get to it!"

"Right, serge," they chorused.

Nick then added, "Serge? Alf? Have we been notified about a motor rally in the area — one that came through last night? I've been getting complaints about noisy and speeding cars."

"No," said Blaketon. "There's been no notification here. But if folks are complaining, Rowan, it's your job to put a stop to the noise and speeding instead of hanging about here discussing football!" and he stalked towards his office.

"Yes, Sergeant," said Nick.

"So get out there and do your duty, Rowan!" was Blaketon's parting shot.

CHAPTER IV

Nick returned to Aidensfield for lunch. He and Kate usually had a light meal, a sandwich perhaps, or an omelette, then if they were both off duty, they enjoyed a more substantial meal in the evening. They might enjoy this at home or as a bar snack in one of the local inns. On this Friday lunch time, however, Nick arrived home ahead of his wife but as he walked into the house, the telephone was ringing. It was the Reverend Jason Chandler, the vicar of Crampton.

"Sorry to bother you at lunch time, Nick," he said. "But somebody's had a go at our offertory box. It's been smashed open and the contents taken."

"Oh, no, not another!" groaned Nick. "How much has gone? Any idea?"

"It's hard to tell, I never know how much there is from day to day, but at a guess, I'd say five or six pounds. That's the usual income around this time of the week."

"There's been a spate of these raids, Mr Chandler," Nick explained. "Something like a couple of dozen in the area during the last few weeks. The thief forces the lid off the boxes with a large screwdriver and steals the cash. Now, have you heard a motorcycle near the church?"

"Yes, when I was having my coffee this morning. I heard it stop somewhere near the church, around eleven o'clock."

"And did you see anyone?"

"Sorry, no," apologised Mr Chandler. "I never suspected anything, not even the motorbike registered any alarm in me."

"If your raid is part of the same series, the raider uses a motorbike to travel to the attacked premises, then forces the offertory boxes by using a large screwdriver with a three-eighths inch blade. It usually leaves marks in the woodwork."

"I'd say this has all the appearance of a similar attack, Nick. What shall I do now?"

"Have a word with your church insurers and consider a new metal cash box which is fitted into the wall of the church; have it cemented in. A local builder will do the job for you. In the meantime, I'll have words with our CID and they'll come to examine the scene, there might be finger-prints on the woodwork and they'll want plaster casts of the break-in marks, to compare it with the others that have been raided. So don't touch anything just yet. I'll come to see you immediately after lunch and I'll make enquiries around Crampton. Somebody might just have been chummy arriving or departing, somebody might just have seen the motor-bike and might recognise it."

And so a new crime was reported. Nick rang Sergeant Blaketon to report the matter and he was far from pleased, exhorting Nick to get out there and catch the thief, other-wise the new inspector would think Ashfordly section officers were a bunch of amateurs. Nick assured Blaketon he'd do everything possible to arrest the thief.

Then before Nick could begin preparation of the lunch, Kate arrived.

"Trouble?" she asked, sensing Nick's mood.

"Another break-in, same method used at Crampton parish church this time. Five or six pounds taken from the offertory box."

"That's awful, Nick, who'd raid churches and steal money like that?"

"If I knew who it was, he'd be arrested in double-quick time and put before the court. I reckon it's somebody fairly local who knows my movements, and those of the other police officers. He always seems to pick a church that's a long way from where we're on duty. And if it is somebody local, somebody who's regularly around in the daytime, his presence wouldn't arouse suspicion, would it?"

"I saw Claude in Ashfordly churchyard this morning," Kate said, walking into the kitchen with Nick following.

"In Ashfordly churchyard?" Nick was surprised. "What was he doing there?"

"Cutting grass," she smiled. "He had a scythe and said he was trimming the long grass around the gravestones. He offered to tend my grandparents' grave."

"And I saw him in Aidensfield churchyard this morning." Nick began to fill the kettle from the tap. "He's obviously getting around them all. He couldn't be our thief, could he?"

"Claude wouldn't break into offertory boxes in churches, Nick, he's not that sort of rogue."

"And he doesn't ride a motorbike," mused Nick. "But I'd better check Aidensfield church again and I'd better have words with him."

"You don't suspect him, surely?" Kate sounded concerned.

"I've got to keep an open mind, love," Nick spoke seriously. "If he's visiting local graveyards, he's up to something dodgy and besides, he might have seen our motor cycling villain."

"You'll have some lunch first?" she smiled. "What do you fancy? A sandwich, or something cooked?"

"A sandwich of some kind will be fine, thanks. I don't have to rush off immediately, there's no desperate urgency about this. I'll ring the CID before I have my sandwich and arrange to meet them at the church."

"Right. Now, when I was in Ashfordly this morning, I bought us a brand-new frying pan, Nick. I want you to be careful with it, no more fires even if nagging women do ring you up! And I got your screwdriver. Three-eighths of an inch blade, as you wanted."

From her shopping bag, she pulled both the pan and the screwdriver. He took the screwdriver and examined it — it was a powerful tool and would make short work of something as flimsy as a wooden offertory box. Just insert the tip of the blade beneath the lid and exert a little pressure . . .

A screwdriver of this size was almost as useful as a jemmy. Who did he know who might possess such a tool, and who also rode a motorbike and who was familiar with the local churches? His mind ranged across the names of several local youngsters who owned motorbikes, but he couldn't imagine any of them being sufficiently evil to raid a church and to take money destined for some charitable purpose. But he was also experienced enough at his job to know that the nicest people are capable of committing crime. The thief could be anyone, someone he knew, someone who appeared honest and decent . . . someone in Aidensfield.

After lunch, he mounted his motorcycle and rode out to the Greengrass ranch. The place was deserted. It was an untidy conglomeration of old farm machinery, motor vehicles, scrap household metal and ruined sheds. Hens clucked among the miasma and a couple of rats scuttled away at his approach. Nick hammered on the door of the weather-battered old house but received no response. He tried the doors, back and front, but both were locked and there was no sign of Alfred either. After shouting Claude's name several times, Nick abandoned this visit. Claude Jeremiah Greengrass was out somewhere.

Nick hoped he wasn't raiding churches.

* * *

Claude was in fact in a churchyard, but he was not stealing money from the offertory box.

He was scything long grass among the tombstones at Ploatby, having received consent from the vicar. As with his other graveyard enterprises, Claude had offered to mow the long grass around the tombstones without making any charge; he said he was tidying the churchyards out of the goodness of his heart, and so the vicar, constantly embarrassed by the untidy state of the graves, had given his consent.

But Claude's mission was not merely to cut grass; he was scrutinising every tombstone, reading the inscriptions and checking names and dates. The grass he was cutting was merely the long strands which obliterated names or dates and, with his razor-sharp scythe, he was able to chop away the intrusive growth to enable him to study the words.

But his endeavour was taking longer than he'd anticipated. He had no idea these small churchyards contained so many graves, they didn't seem to be arranged in any particular sequence or order and so he walked miles, trudging around the stones, chopping down the grass, reading the names . . . and all the time, Alfred followed him, patient and loyal to his master.

"If he's buried here, I'm going to find him, Alfred," he said to the dog on more than one occasion. "Come on, it's time to go a bit further!"

* * *

For Graham Blaketon and his mother, the drive across the North York Moors from Pickering to Aidensfield had been beautiful.

With staggering views of the open moorland, offset with deep tree-lined valleys and tiny villages, Graham had manoeuvred the vehicle up the hills and around the corners without any problems. They'd taken several detours off the main road to provide Graham with more experience, and he'd even negotiated the steep downward incline of the Devil's Elbow at the Hole of Horcum without causing his mother undue anguish!

He'd shown that he was a very capable young driver; en route, they'd stopped for a meal at one of the moorland pubs and had even taken a stroll along one of the more scenic of the moorland footpaths. When they arrived at Aidensfield, it was mid-afternoon and they received a warm welcome from Mrs Rhoda Myers, Denis' mother. In her mid-forties, she was a comely country woman who welcomed everyone to her home as if they were long-time friends.

A kettle was singing on the hob and she had prepared some buttered scones with strawberry jam. After the preliminaries, during which she showed Graham the bedroom he would occupy, they all sat down for a cup of tea and some scones. They chattered about old times, when the boys had been at school together and laughed at some of their escapades, and then it was time for Joan to leave.

"I must be going, Rhoda," Joan smiled. "I promised Margaret I'd be there before four o'clock. It's so good of you to let Graham come for the weekend."

"It's a real pleasure, Joan, I really mean it. Denis hasn't many friends in the village now, they've grown up and moved away, or else they've got cars so I'm so pleased he and Graham keep in touch."

Graham stood up as his mother was preparing to leave. "Mum, I haven't got a present for Dad yet. I'll be seeing him on Saturday night, we're going out for a meal together."

"He'll be so pleased about that!" she smiled.

"I wondered if you could get something in Whitby for him, from me. Then, when you come back this way tomorrow, you could drop it in here, I'm sure Mrs Myers will be in."

"I won't be far away, Joan, if I'm not around, just leave it in the wash-house."

"All right," agreed Joan. "I'll see if I can find something from both of us. I'm returning home late on Saturday afternoon so I'll come around this way and drop it off. You'll be going home on Sunday, Graham?"

"Yes, I'll get the bus back, don't worry about me."

And Graham pulled a £1 note from his pocket and passed it to his mother. "Here, this will be my share."

"All right, see you tomorrow perhaps, 'bye!" and she left the Myers' house. Graham watched her leave, waving as she turned the corner to head out of Aidensfield towards Whitby, and then returned to his hostess.

"So what are you two doing tonight?" asked Mrs Myers. "It's Killing Pits Club night," said Denis. "I thought me and Graham should go, we used to go as kids!"

"Great idea!" enthused Graham. "We used to race our bikes up and down the green, didn't we? Then some of them got motorbikes and scrambled over the moors . . ."

"It's all cars now," said Denis wistfully. "I can't join because I haven't a car, but we can go along to have a look . . . it's great fun, there's some really smart cars there. And some old bangers souped up! Gordon's got an Austin Healey . . ."

Mrs Myers left the pair to plan their evening while she began to clear the table. It was so nice that Denis had a friend to stay — he had seemed a bit lonesome lately. All the other village lads had managed to buy themselves a car, but the wages Denis got as an apprentice bricklayer didn't allow him to spend that sort of money. He was saving up for a car, she knew, and sooner or later, he'd be able to afford one.

Then he'd be one of the gang again.

* * *

It was around six o'clock that same evening, Friday, that Graham and Denis went outside the house and into the garage. Denis was planning to show Graham his motorcycle, but Graham's eyes lighted on the car which was parked beside it. It was an old Austin A40 in a rusty condition, almost a banger in fact, and it bore "L" plates.

"Who's is the car?" asked Graham.

"It's Dad's," Denis explained. "He's away at sea a lot, he comes home once every five or six weeks, and he's supposed to be teaching me to drive. That's why it's got "L" plates on.

But he's never here, and when he does come home he never seems to have time to help me. And mum can't drive, so she can't accompany me. There's no driving schools around here, so I'm stuck. I'm never going to learn how to drive a car!"

"I'm a passed driver now," Graham boasted. "I drove all the way here, in mum's car. I could accompany you, as your passed driver, at least for this weekend."

Denis' face brightened. "Yeh, you could, eh! We could take the car to the Killing Pits tonight, eh? And do the run, me driving and you beside me . . ."

"Could we?"

"Yeh, course we could! They won't let me join the club now, 'cos I haven't a car. I'm not allowed. I can't do the run, can't do anything . . . I mean, there's a car here, not being used and the club's meeting tonight. It seems daft not to take the car down to the village tonight, and join the Killing Pits Club run . . . ."

"Would she let us take it? I mean, would your mum really allow me to supervise you driving?"

"We could always ask," Denis didn't sound very sure about his mother's reaction to that idea, but as they were pondering that suggestion, Mrs Myers came into the back yard to hang out some washing.

She saw them and realised they were plotting some scheme; smiling, she asked, "Now then, you two, what are you scheming?"

Denis looked at Graham, and Graham looked at Denis, neither wishing to be the one to pose the question. But as Graham realised that Denis would never pluck up the courage, he took a deep breath and said, "Er, Mrs Myers. I'm a passed driver now, I drove all the way here from Pickering and, well, I was wondering . . ."

She anticipated his question. "You were wondering whether you could borrow the car, eh? You and our Denis?"

"Well, yes."

Denis added, "Can we mum, just for tonight?"

It was evident that she was far from enthusiastic but she did not like to offend the guest by an outright refusal. "Well, I suppose so," she condescended. "After all, Graham is the sergeant's son and he won't do anything silly, will you, Graham?"

"No, I won't, I know how to behave . . . we'll not drink and drive, Mrs Myers, and I'll look after the car."

"Well, in that case, I suppose you can borrow it. But our Denis mustn't drive. You're just a learner, our Denis, and I know your dad wouldn't allow it. But because Graham's passed his test, he can drive. That's what I say — Graham must be the driver. Now, the car doesn't go far these days, Dad says it could do with more outings . . . yes, all right. Mind, I'm relying on you to look after things, Graham."

"I will, I promise," smiled Graham Blaketon.

But she didn't miss the smile of triumph on the face of her son.

CHAPTER V

Having secured the necessary screwdriver, Nick decided he could complete his work on the MG, hopefully in one session that Friday evening. He finished his patrol duties around five thirty, one annoyingly unresolved enquiry being the identity of the raider of Crampton church. Another concern was the continuing absence, from his usual haunts, of Claude Jeremiah Greengrass. Nick had been to his scruffy moorland home on several occasions during the day, but each time Claude had been absent, and Nick had not spotted the rogue anywhere around Aidensfield either. He was telling Kate about it.

"I can't think where he's got to, he's usually somewhere about the place during the afternoons," he said as they enjoyed a meal cooked in their new frying pan.

"You don't honestly think he's the guilty person, Nick?" Kate asked him. "He just wouldn't do that sort of thing. Claude would never go into a church to steal money by breaking into offertory boxes."

"No, and he hasn't got a motorbike either," Nick mused. "I don't really suspect him, but I must interview him. He is going around local churchyards, and it is local churches that are being raided. It's very feasible he could have seen the culprit, even if he didn't realise it. If Blaketon ever finds out I've *not* grilled Claude, I'll get it in the neck!"

"Sergeant Blaketon seems to think Claude's guilty of every crime that occurs around here," smiled Kate. "The poor old chap can't win, can he? Even when he's doing someone a good turn, he's suspected of being up to no good!"

"The first thing Blaketon said to me when I was posted to Aidensfield was "Keep an eye on Claude Jeremiah Greengrass". He went on at great length about what a villain he was, but I know Claude's not that sort of villain, Kate. A rogue yes, but never a break-in merchant. Even so, if I don't interrogate him and find out everything he can tell me and eliminate him from our enquiries, Blaketon will say I'm not doing my job, he'll hint that I'm neglecting my duties!"

"So you haven't told Sergeant Blaketon about Claude's visits to those churchyards?" Kate grinned at him. "That means you don't really suspect Claude."

"If I'd mentioned Claude's visits to those churchyards with some cock-and-bull story about cutting grass, Blaketon would have him locked-up for questioning! But I can wait — Claude'll turn up sooner or later."

"Nick, we talked about going out tonight but I've got some paperwork to do, I'm working at Whitby tomorrow. Jim Radcliffe is having the weekend off — a family wedding I think."

Kate had recently formed a surgery partnership with Doctor James Radcliffe of Whitby, the pair of them setting up a joint practice in the town. Kate's Aidensfield practice had been linked to the Whitby one.

This amalgamation had produced a larger, more efficient unit. The new arrangements meant Kate would have more time off because Radcliffe would cover Aidensfield and district in her absence. For the two doctors, the scheme was working well, even if some of the patients were taking their time in making adjustments.

"I'm working in Whitby too," grinned Nick. "Football duties tomorrow. Me, Alf Ventress and Blaketon. I'm being picked up here at one o'clock. That means I can have Saturday night off which means I'll definitely be able to get my car exhaust fixed!"

"You're not spending Saturday night lying under a dirty old car!" she retorted. "You can do it tonight while I'm busy with my paperwork! Then we can have Saturday night off, we might even go out for a bar snack or something!"

"Right, great idea! I should get the exhaust fitted tonight. Once I get that awkward bracket shifted, it won't take long to fix the new one."

And so, after they'd finished their meal and washed up the pots, Nick changed into his overalls and went into the garage. The new exhaust was lying on the floor and so he lay on his back and eased his way beneath the jacked-up MG, his new screwdriver to hand. And he breathed a sigh of relief as the power exerted through it enabled him to free the stubborn bracket. He removed it very quickly and realised that fitting the new part would be now a comparatively simple task.

He began to whistle as he worked.

* * *

As Nick worked happily in his garage, members of the Killing Pits Club were gathering upon the grassy portion of moorland at the end of the village. It was dark by this time — around nine o'clock — and some eight or nine cars had assembled. They were truly an assorted lot — one or two were smart sports cars but some were old bangers of doubtful safety, many with rusted bodywork and unsafe lighting systems or unreliable engines. Their spare parts were obtained from scrap yards and some of the cars functioned through a combination of good luck and wishful thinking!

Wandering among them were several teenage youths and girls, eighteen or twenty in total, all aged between seventeen and nineteen. They were generating a good deal of noise too. Engines were being revved, radios were being played, sometimes a horn would blast or there would be an outburst of laughter or giggling as the young men chased girls around the cars and across the moor into the heather and bracken. But at this deserted location, there were few houses and so no one complained.

The Killing Pits Club had met at this venue for as long as any member of the gathering could recall, first with bicycles and then with motorbikes, and none of the villagers had complained.

Although the very young children of Aidensfield continued to meet here to play after school, these maturing youngsters had cars and they continued to meet at the same place. It had long been the play-area for the village children, their own portion of moorland. And it was known as the Killing Pits.

The reason for this odd name was lost in history. The edge of the moor at this point was covered with short grass, shorn beautifully by the ever-present free-roaming moorland sheep, but as the moor rose gradually from the road, the terrain became rougher. It developed into a mass of shallow ditches and uneven bumps, many hidden beneath the heather and bracken, and some historians believed this was the site of the early village. From time to time, Stone Age artefacts were found and bones had been discovered in the early eighteenth century. The earthworks were probably the remains of buildings, long since fallen into ruin and buried, and it was possible to identify moats, walls, floor spaces, doorways and so forth.

Another theory was that the site had been used, probably in Stone Age times, to trap wild animals. Deep pits were dug in the moorland and wild animals, such as deer or even wolves, were driven into them. The hunters would arrange themselves around the higher edges of the pits and once the animals were trapped, they would systematically be killed with spears or even heavy rocks. Hence the name — Killing Pits.

For the young children of Aidensfield, however, the entire area, a moorland space without boundaries or fences, was a haven of delight. The pits were pits no longer but merely shallow depressions in the earth and here the youngsters could play without danger and without hindrance, as they had for centuries. Even now, the children of Aidensfield relaxed at the Killing Pits, playing hide and seek among the tall bracken in the summer, tobogganing in the winter or simply meeting there to decide what else to do.

Many of the older children, now teenagers, had cars. This was the adult section of the Killing Pits Club and membership was strictly limited to those who owned a motor car. Those who had access to a car, such as the family saloon, did not qualify. Youths had therefore stretched themselves financially in order to purchase a motor car, any sort of motor car, because membership of the Killing Pits Club was indeed a matter of some stature. Only the best of Aidensfield and district could join!

And so it was, in the darkness of that late evening, that the present generation of senior Killing Pits Club members gathered for a meeting. Their leader was Gordon Turnbull. No one had elected Gordon but he was a natural leader. His style, his free spending of money, his well-paid job, his commanding presence and his natural qualities of leadership had all combined to make him the obvious choice. And the others followed him, almost without question.

Tonight, however, he was having problems. The engine of his Austin Healey was overheating, apparently through a leak in the radiator, and if this was the case he could not give the vehicle a time trial tonight. Indeed, it must not go anywhere because the engine could seize up — and that would be extremely costly. He had the bonnet up now and was peering into the radiator with a torch. The water level was very low, far lower than was safe even though he had topped it up before leaving home. As he searched around the engine, he saw the tell-tale signs of glistening water on the grass beneath. He cursed to himself — it was a very severe leak and it would have to be fixed. He shouted to his girlfriend, Julie, who was in the driving seat.

"Start her up, Julie, and give her a short burst while I listen . . ."

His girlfriend obeyed, switching on the ignition and pressing the accelerator as Gordon's keen hearing tried to identify any unwelcome sounds from the engine. But it seemed to be running sweetly; the ignition system seemed fine, none of the plugs was missing a sequence of firing. So far, no real harm seemed to have been done.

"OK, Julie, switch off. It's overheating, that's what's making it miss sometimes. There's a radiator leak. So we're grounded tonight."

She switched off the engine and came around to him as he closed the bonnet.

"So we won't be doing the run tonight?" she asked.

"Not you and me, not in this car anyway, but the others can do a circuit. Hello, here comes young Blaketon and that chump, Denis Myers!"

Gordon grinned as the battered old A40 with Graham Blaketon at the wheel, eased to a halt at the edge of the group. The car was bearing "L" plates, and so Gordon went over to greet Graham.

"Graham! Nice to see you," they shook hands. "So what brings you back to Aidensfield?"

"I'm staying with Denis for the weekend, my mum's in Whitby so I came along for the outing. So the Killing Pits Club's still very active, eh?"

"Lively and popular, that's the description. So is this your car?"

"No, it belongs to Denis' dad, Denis is the learner. I've passed my test, but I haven't a car of my own yet. Anyway, we thought we'd come and see what goes on here!"

"You did right," then Gordon placed his fingers between his lips and produced a loud, piercing whistle. It had the desired effect — everyone stopped to listen to him.

"Hey, everybody, Graham's here," and several of them shouted "Hi Graham" and other words of greeting. As one or two came across to speak to Graham Blaketon, Gordon turned to Denis. His manner was condescending and he spoke with just a hint of a sneer.

"So, our Denis, you still haven't got your own car?"

"No, I can't afford one, Gordon, not yet. I'm saving up though, earning bits of extra cash wherever I can. But I wondered if I could join now though, and do the run tonight in this car. It's my dad's and I can drive it, with Graham accompanying me."

"No chance!" echoed Gordon. "You know the rules, our Denis. Only *owners* of cars can join."

"But you're letting Graham in!"

"As my guest. As the guest of a club member who must have a car. Besides, he's the sergeant's son, we might need him, if you see what I mean. He might be able to exert a bit of influence if we happen to need it . . ."

Graham, who'd been chatting to another of the members, did not hear the exchange, but was now coming to rejoin Denis and Gordon.

"So Denis will be doing the run tonight, Gordon?" asked Graham.

"No chance, Graham, he can't. Sorry and all that, but it's the rules."

The look on Denis' face indicated his disappointment but he said nothing. One day he'd show that pompous Gordon Turnbull . . . one day he *would* have a car and one day he would arrive in a posh sports car with a lovely girl beside him . . . one day . . .

"Tell you what, our Denis," smiled Gordon. "You can be the timekeeper for tonight. How about that? It is an important duty."

Rather than be left out of the evening's entertainment, Denis agreed. He would wave the cars off and see them back, entering their times on a piece of paper to determine who was the slowest tonight. And the slowest would have to buy drinks for all the others at the Aidensfield Arms after the run. He hoped Gordon was slowest — the slow worm, the slowest was called. He'd love to see Gordon as the slow worm . . .

Then Gordon whistled through his fingers once more, the shrill sound compelling everyone to a respectful silence.

"Right everybody," he shouted. "Time for action. Our Denis is going to be the timekeeper, so it's a case of drawing lots for the running order."

"It's been done," said somebody from the darkness.

"Good, we are highly organised! So who's first?"

A youth called Ian raised his hand. "Me and Liz," he called back.

"Right, get to your starting place. We set off at one-minute intervals. No short cuts allowed. Norman's the half-way marshal, so you must pass him during the circuit. And the slowest is the slow worm for tonight and he buys the first round for everybody. Right, our Denis? Got a white handkerchief and a watch?"

Denis showed his wristwatch and waved his handkerchief as Gordon indicated the starting point. Graham walked beside Denis and said, "I'll come with you, Denis, I'm not doing the circuit, not in your dad's car. I promised to look after it."

"Thanks," said Denis, who then saw Ian and Liz heading his way. He held out his arm to halt them at the starting point, checked his watch and said, "Ready?"

Ian, in a tiny Hillman Imp, shouted from the window.

"Ready and waiting, Denis!"

Denis began to study his watch and raised the white handkerchief. "OK, ready, Ian? Get set. Five, four, three, two, one. Go!"

And with a roar of its engine, the gallant little car raced from the Killing Pits and headed for Aidensfield village.

"Next one take your position," shouted Denis and a sporty Triumph Spitfire moved forward.

* * *

At the Aidensfield Arms, George Ward, the landlord, was polishing glasses. The bar was deserted and he was beginning to wonder where his customers were when the door crashed open and in staggered Claude Jeremiah Greengrass.

He was carrying a scythe and a strickle, and had Alfred at the end of a long lead. As man and dog entered the bar, the scythe crashed against the tables and chairs, banged the counter and threatened to demolish the peaceful state of the inn as Claude made for the counter.

He was hobbling painfully and looked completely exhausted. He puffed and wheezed as he tried to deposit the scythe against the counter.

"Now you've got in without wrecking the place, Claude, I take it you'll be having your usual?"

"I need summat that fortifies the over-fifties and stops me feet aching!" breathed Claude. "By, I've had a rough day!"

"Well, start with a pint — and have this one on the house. It might bring us both good luck — where is everybody?"

"Shall I go out and come in again?" blinked Claude. "That'll make it two customers!"

"And you'll be expecting two free pints! No chance. Anyway, you look shattered! Been busy, have you?" George wondered what on earth Claude had been doing. He was seldom this late into the pub and he never looked so worn out.

"Busy?" echoed Claude. "Folks round here don't know the meaning of the word. I've never seen so many gravestones!" and at that point, they were interrupted by the roar of a car as it hurtled past the pub.

"Somebody leaving his wife, is it?" smiled Claude.

"It's them daft lads again, the Killing Pits Club. Racing around the village, they are. They'll be killing somebody next . . . I don't know why Nick doesn't put a stop to it."

"He couldn't put a stop to a leaking tap!" grinned Claude.

"They wait till he's off duty, then they race around the moor. Slowest one on the night has to buy drinks all round."

"Free drinks all round?" beamed Claude. "Then I'll wait!"

"They'll be coming in soon so you'd better shift that scythe. I don't want anybody getting hurt!"

"I'll sit down near the fire," smiled Claude. "I can wait . . . come on, Alfred," but Alfred's lead was tangled around a chair leg and it fell over as the dog moved.

"Claude, you'll be paying for damages if you're not careful!"

"Aye, well, I might just be able to pay up an' all, I'm likely to come into money, George, big money, so think on who you're talking to," grinned Claude, his eyes blinking furiously.

CHAPTER VI

That same Friday evening, Nick was determined to complete the work on his car. The new screwdriver had enabled him to dispose of the stubborn bracket and once that had been dealt with, it was a comparatively simple matter to fit the new system. As he was making the final adjustments, Kate came to see how he was progressing.

"Five more minutes, love," he shouted from beneath the vehicle. "Then it's done! It'll sound as sweet as a sewing machine!"

"Shall I make us a drink?" she asked. "I've finished my paperwork."

"How about a drink at the pub instead? I feel like a long cool pint after working among all this dust and dirt."

"All right, I'd enjoy that. I'll run a bath for you."

"And you can jump in with me!" he shouted as he emerged from beneath. "Lots of warm water and bubbles."

"I've had my bath!" she said rather coldly. "And besides, who'd want to share a bath with a man who looks as if he's just finished a shift in an oil well?"

And she left him to his work. He slid under the car, tugged at the exhaust to make sure it was secure then began to tighten each of the securing bolts. Just before the final tightening he'd run the engine to ensure there were no leaks. It was during a moment of silence as he shifted position that he heard the roar of a car engine outside; he listened carefully, trying to determine from the noise whether or not the vehicle was racing or merely passing. But it did sound like a speeding car . . . he waited. If this was like last night, there'd be another along in a minute.

And so there was. With a roaring of its engine and a squealing of its tyres, another vehicle hurtled through Aidensfield and so Nick decided he must do something about this. If there were no rallies, it was probably local youths and he knew they must be stopped. Perhaps his visit to the pub tonight would be very timely?

* * *

Inside the police house, Kate had prepared a couple of mugs of coffee and was waiting for Nick to arrive when the telephone rang. She was tempted to ignore it, with both Nick and she being off duty, but she relented. It could be someone needing urgent help.

"Dr Rowan, Aidensfield Police House," she announced.

"It's Jack Wilson here," snapped the angry voice. "Is your husband in?"

"Not at the moment, Mr Wilson, he's off duty this evening, so can I take a message?"

And at that instance, a terrible roaring noise sounded in the garage; Nick was running the engine of his MG and pressing the accelerator to test his new exhaust pipe.

The din echoed in the confines of the garage and because she'd left the door open, the noise also filled the house.

She shouted into the telephone.

"I'm sorry, Mr Wilson, what was the message?"

"It's those noisy cars!" bellowed the caller. "I can hear 'em now. Racing through the village, they are, creating a terrible racket and going far too fast. They're a liability, Dr Rowan, somebody'll get hurt one of these days. I want your husband to do something about them, put a stop to whatever they're doing, make sure decent residents have a chance of a bit of peace and quiet. Then there's the danger aspect, you know, the speed some of 'em are going."

"Yes, I'm sure he will deal with the matter when he gets back on duty, Mr Wilson. He is aware of the problem and I do know he is making enquiries to trace the perpetrators." And as she spoke, the noise stopped. Nick had switched off his engine and the resultant silence was a blessed relief but Kate was still shouting! She was speaking in a false raised voice to Mr Wilson before she realised it was quiet around her.

"There you are," said the caller. "That's what we have to put up with all the time, dozens of 'em racing past our house. Mark my words, there'll be an accident one of these days . . ."

"I'll ask Nick to contact you about it," she said sweetly just as he came into the room, wiping his hands on an oily rag. She replaced the handset with a smile.

"Who was that?" Nick asked her. "A call-out?"

"No," she said sternly. "It was Jack Wilson from just along the street, he's complaining about noisy cars, and if you'd heard the racket you were making . . ."

"It works perfectly," he enthused. "No more fumes leaking through, no more illegal noise . . . I've done a good job in there! I could always get a job as a mechanic if I leave the Force!"

"I think the residents want you to do an even better job by stopping those noisy cars outside!"

"When I get back on duty," he said. "That will be my first priority — after I've caught the offertory box thief. Now, a quick coffee, a quick bath and a trip to the pub for a quick pint! We'll have to get there before George closes. I can't walk in after time and ask for a drink!"

* * *

Nick was bathed and ready in less than ten minutes and when he and Kate entered the pub, it was deserted except for Claude Jeremiah Greengrass and Alfred. Claude was sitting at a table with Alfred at his feet and an almost empty pint glass before him. George was alone at the bar counter too, amusing himself with a crossword puzzle in the local paper. The inn was desperately quiet and so, when Nick and Kate walked in, George beamed with pleasure.

"Customers!" he smiled a welcome. "You know, I was beginning to think I'd got smelly breath or something. It's been dead quiet these last two evenings. Anyway, nice to see you. So what can I get you both?"

"A gin and tonic for Kate and a pint for me, George. And one for yourself. So what's the matter with old Claude? He's not his usual chirpy self, is he?" Nick could see the tiredness in both Claude and Alfred.

"He's worn himself out, Nick — and Alfred! The pair of them have been trudging around graveyards. Claude reckons he's been cutting grass; it seems he's got a sudden desire to cut grass in every churchyard for miles around but why he's doing it remains a mystery. And on top of that, he's broke, he's been sat with that single pint all night! It's not the happiest of sights, is it? Seeing Claude like that?"

"He's not actually working, is he?" grinned Nick. "The mere thought of that would wear him out and it would make him as miserable as sin!"

"He reckons he's cutting out of the goodness of his heart, it's his civic duty or something," responded George.

"He's up to something, George. He'd never exert himself like that, not without any pay or reward. He's definitely up to something that's a secret and the crafty old blighter isn't telling anybody what it is."

"He tore an article or an advert out of my *Gazette* last night," volunteered George. "I've no idea what it was about, though, because I hadn't had a chance to read it before he ripped it to pieces! And he never even said thanks."

"So he's got some scheme going, eh?" reckoned Nick. "I'll bet it's some plot designed to make him a bit of cash!"

"Nick, you are awful!" Kate interrupted them. "You know he's just cutting grass, tidying graveyards and clearing rubbish. He's doing it out of the goodness of his heart!"

"Claude never does anything out of the goodness of his heart!" Nick was emphatic. "He'll pretend he's doing it out of kindness to his fellow creatures, but he's broke, I happen to know that. He's after making some easy cash, Kate, and I'm curious to know how. So, I'll get him a drink, I want to talk to him."

"Nick!" breathed Kate. "You're off duty! Relax!"

"If I don't catch him for a quick word now, I might not see him for weeks, especially if he's rushing around more churchyards," and with that, Nick turned to Claude and called across to him. "The usual, Claude?"

The lonely, tired Claude glanced up and managed to raise a flicker of a smile. "What's the catch, Constable?"

"Catch? There isn't a catch! There doesn't have to be a catch if I offer to buy you a drink," smiled Nick.

"If my feet weren't killing me, and if I wasn't broke, I'd never accept a drink from a copper."

"So there's a time to break your own rules," grinned Nick.

"Well," said Claude. "There comes a time when honourable blokes like me have to swallow their pride, so I'll have a pint."

Kate smiled at Claude.

"Nick's celebrating, he's got the exhaust fixed on his old car."

"And to think I let him have the car at a bargain price," grumbled Claude. "I was robbed! By a man of the law, an' all. I could have made a fortune from that car on the open market, once I'd got it done up!"

"So have a pint as compensation," chuckled Nick. "Anyway, it sounds as sweet as a trombone now."

As George was organising the drinks, Claude said, "While you're talking about noisy exhausts, Constable, has anybody complained about those lads racing past? They'll be doing somebody some harm one of these days. You ought to be out there nicking 'em instead of spending time in the pub!"

"I'm off duty, Claude. Even village constables need time off, you know. Anyway, that noise didn't come from a motor rally," said Nick. "I've checked."

"I know it didn't come from a motor rally!" snapped Claude, coming to the bar to accept his pint. "It's them daft kids, young Thornton and his gang. Killing Pits Club. They've no sense, racing through the street like that. Me and Alfred had to leap for our lives the other day, going like hell they were . . . car after car . . ."

"What's these Killing Pits, then?" asked Nick as Kate accepted her drink.

"Village kids have played there for years, Nick. It's some old earthworks on the moor, at the far end of the village, just beyond the church. Stone Age man used to drive wild animals into pits they'd dug on the moor, and then kill them. Traps, they were. Very effective. Some experts say they're not old pits but the remains of a Stone Age village. Anyway, whatever they are, they've always been called the Killing Pits and kids have always played there, little kids and big kids. The pits are quite safe now, they're not deep or dangerous, but the land around them is ridged and furrowed, full of hiding places when the bracken's high. It's a lovely play-area, but these lads with cars meet there and call themselves the Killing Pits Club."

"So it's those lads who are racing through the village, creating complaints?" Nick realised.

"Aye," said Claude. "Round and round they go, like bats out of hell. It's time you put a stop to 'em, before somebody gets killed."

"It's not so much the noise, Nick," said George, accepting Nick's money. "But you know what lads are, they race around a circuit, on a time trial basis, and the slowest one has to buy drinks all round when they come in here. Sometimes they'll do three circuits or three separate trials. Slowest out of three runs, averaging all their times, has to buy the others their drinks. It's bound to make them take chances, to cut corners and take risks, and that can only lead to dangerous driving."

"You're right, of course," replied Nick. "I'll look into the matter and put a stop to it. There were some cars earlier tonight but they seem to have stopped now."

"That means they'll be in here any minute now!" breathed George. "I'd better get myself organised for a big order." Claude took his drink across to the table he'd been occupying and so Nick followed; Kate joined them as Nick settled opposite his old adversary.

"Here!" protested Claude. "Just because I allow the law to buy me a drink doesn't mean I want to be seen drinking with the law!"

"There's nobody here to see us, Claude," smiled Nick. "So, this grass cutting enterprise of yours . . ."

"I knew there was a catch!"

"Come on, Claude, you're up to something!"

"Me? You've a nasty suspicious mind, Constable. Here am I, doing a favour for the village and you think I'm pinching it!"

"Pinching what?" Nick asked.

"Grass!" laughed Claude. "You think I'm pinching grass to sell for feeding pet rabbits . . ."

"Claude, this is serious." Nick realised he'd been led into a trap that time. "Someone's raiding offertory boxes."

Claude reacted. "Now we're getting down to it! You're accusing me of thieving, eh? You think I'm raiding those boxes while I'm cutting grass!"

"No, I don't, Claude! I told you that last time," Nick tried to calm the situation. "But I do think you might have seen somebody around while you've been working. Somebody sneaking in to carry out those raids. That's what I'm after — the identity of the real thief!"

Claude took a deep breath. "Well, that's put it straight enough. Now, I'm no grass but I happen to think I'm respectable enough not to rob churches. I reckon that folks who rob charities and churches are real villains. Now, as it happens, I have heard a motorbike, but I saw nothing because I was working a long way from the church doors, you see, in the rough at the far end of the churchyards, more often than not. And I never go into churches with mucky boots on, so I never saw a soul . . . never saw a soul! Good that, eh? Witty! I'm a witty sort of chap you know, I could have been a comedian, doing the clubs. Never saw a soul in church, that's clever stuff!"

"Very funny, Claude," agreed Nick with reluctance. "But did you see the motorbike at all?"

Claude shook his head. "No, not once. I mean, I'm not looking out for trouble, you know, not when I'm cutting grass!"

"So, Claude, let's get back to basic, back to this grass cutting business. I'm intrigued about it, about your plans and way of working . . ."

But at that moment, the door of the pub crashed open and a noisy crowd of youngsters began to press into the bar. Youths and girls surged forward.

Nick recognised Graham Blaketon among them. Kate noticed Denis Myers too, but it was Gordon Turnbull who was first in the queue.

"Evening, George. The usual for the Killing Pits Club. That's nine pints to start with, four gin and tonics . . ." and then he noticed Nick and Kate.

"Ah," he halted his order and said, "we have the law in tonight, eh? Good evening Constable Rowan, Doctor Rowan, Claude. Can I get you all a drink?"

"Aye!" interrupted Claude. "You can, mine's a pint!"

"For you, Claude, I shall be pleased. Mr and Mrs Rowan?" Nick immediately recognised an opportunity to speak to these youngsters about their jaunts from the Killing Pits and so he asked for a pint of bitter, with a gin and tonic for Kate.

Gordon Turnbull, eager to remain in the limelight, shouted to the others. "I'm paying tonight, I'm feeling generous. George, get whatever the others want."

And as George worked on the order, Gordon came across to Nick and seated himself at the table.

"How's that car of yours, Mr Rowan? You ought to join our club, you know. We've some beautiful cars, our members have a bit of style. Well, some of them have."

"You're not holding races or time trials around the moors, are you, Gordon? You and your Killing Pits Club?"

"We wouldn't even consider it, Constable!"

Nick allowed that remark to pass. "It's illegal, you know, running motor vehicle races or time trials on a public highway. And if you organise such a rally, you must notify the police and provide precise details of the route, the time and date, the number of contestants — with a limit of a hundred in some cases — and so forth, and your contestants must obey all the rules of the road including speed limits while the rally is operating."

Gordon smiled smoothly at Nick. "We'd never break the law, Mr Rowan, that's a cardinal rule of our club. We never drink before we drive, and tonight one driver in every car will have a soft drink. We're very keen to obey the law."

"I have been getting complaints about noisy cars speeding through Aidensfield," Nick told him.

"Then it must be some other organisation," said Gordon. "Rest assured it's not us, Mr Rowan!"

And with that remark, Gordon rose from his chair and bade them enjoy their drinks while he rejoined his companions.

Claude looked at Nick.

"Smooth talking young sod!" he grumbled.

"I'll keep an eye open for them, Claude," Nick assured him.

* * *

That night in the Myers household, Graham Blaketon was preparing for bed. He was sharing a room with Denis, each occupying a single bed in the back bedroom.

As Graham changed into his pyjamas, he glanced across the room towards Denis. Denis was in his own single bed in the sparsely furnished bedroom and Graham saw him pick up a bottle of pills from his bedside cabinet and swallow one. The act of taking the pill was aided by a drink from a glass of water.

"Are you ill or something?" Graham asked, with a hint of concern in his voice.

"I've got this rash," said Denis, and he rolled up his pyjama sleeve for Graham to see his arms. "It's an allergy, so the doctor says. I've got to take these pills."

"It's not something catching, is it?" asked Graham, just a little worried.

"No, it'll soon clear up. These pills are good. They're pretty powerful, mind. The doctor says I've not to drive after taking them, and I can't drink either, I can't even have one alcoholic drink. And she's signed me off for a week!"

"So that's why you were drinking tomato juices! Well, so long as I don't catch it!"

"No, there's no fear of that. Well, I'm going to crash out now, I'm shattered."

"Me too," said Graham, thinking over Gordon's refusal to allow poor Denis to run around the circuit. "Goodnight."

"See you tomorrow," said Denis sliding between the sheets.

"Mum might let us borrow the car again, tomorrow," said Denis. "Then we could have a real nice outing, eh?"

CHAPTER VII

Having thoroughly enjoyed Terence Rattigan's *Separate Tables* at Whitby Spa Theatre that Friday evening with Margaret, Joan Forrester spent Saturday morning alone in the town. She wanted to do a little sightseeing, particularly around the harbourside and along the piers, but she also had some shopping to complete. Margaret was unable to accompany her that morning because she was at work — she worked in a building society office in Baxtergate which closed at one o'clock. As a consequence, Joan was alone to enjoy her morning in Whitby's quaint old streets.

Her primary task was to find a suitable birthday present for Oscar. Even though they'd been divorced for some years now, she always tried to remember his birthday and always sent him a card at Christmas, along with a small gift. At times, he seemed so very much alone because he'd never formed a new relationship with a woman. Although he was dour and at times humourless, Joan knew that Oscar still cared deeply for both her and Graham.

So far as a present was concerned, she had no idea what to buy, except that it must be something from both she and Graham but as she strolled around the old streets she found a delightful second-hand bookshop in Silver Street. That reminded her of his love of the Bronte novels.

Oscar collected specialist editions of the books and had accumulated a very comprehensive selection. Joan decided that a Bronte novel, particularly *Wuthering Heights*, would be ideal if it was an edition he did not have. She realised she was unsure of the current situation with his collection, but decided to visit the shop.

Joan spent some time browsing along the shelves of musty old volumes and then, almost like a miracle, she found a battered old copy of *Wuthering Heights*. Pulling it carefully from the shelf, she turned the cover and, with hands quivering, realised it was one of the first Blackamoor editions. First editions were always sought after, even though a collector might have several — they could be used for bartering, for swopping for other volumes or even for sale. They always brought a good price. The shop assistant, a small man with a rounded face beneath a head of smooth shiny skin, came from the rear of his premises and noticed Joan holding the book.

"A very rare copy, madam," he said. "Very collectable. It's one we got in from a house clearance, the only Bronte novel in the entire house. It's a pity the others were not there too. That one arrived yesterday in fact; it went on the shelves only this morning!"

"Is it very expensive?" she asked.

"I'm asking £10 for that one," he said. "It's lower than some similar volumes because the spine needs expert attention but I suppose £10 is rather a lot."

Joan knew that a good hardback novel cost around 12s. 6d at that time which made the Bronte book seem expensive, but she knew it would increase in value.

"I'll take it," she smiled. "It's for my ex-husband, a present from me and our son."

"A wise purchase, madam. Shall I wrap it?" offered the shopkeeper.

"Thank you, that would be nice."

"And I do have gift tags," offered the little fellow as he opened a drawer and passed one to Joan. While he wrapped the novel in brown paper and string, Joan began to write her message on the tag.

* * *

While Joan was enjoying her morning in Whitby, Nick was patrolling the villages around Aidensfield, calling at all the churches to check the security of their offertory boxes. Elsinby, Ploatby, Craydale, Briggsby, Brantgate, Waindale, Falconbridge, Fieldholme, Whemmelby and Gelderslack — he arranged his route to include each of these small communities, some in very isolated locations. Happily, none of the offertory boxes had been broken into and he logged each visit in his official notebook. In those cases where there was a resident vicar, he paid a call to remind him that a thief was touring the villages and preying on the contents of those small wooden boxes. He sought extra vigilance from the vicars and congregations, and all promised their co-operation.

He knew that his presence in the villages would have been noticed by the residents and if the thief was a person from any of these communities, that might just act as a deterrent. Word of police interest would rapidly spread.

While Nick was executing his duty by calling at all the village churches, so Claude Jeremiah Greengrass was going about his own lawfully imposed task by doing likewise, albeit not in the same sequence or at the same time. Armed with his scythe and strickle, and with Alfred in attendance, his first call that morning was at Stovensby, and his next was at Thackerston.

At Stovensby, he tied the unprotesting Alfred to a tree as he began a tour of the older tombstones, inspecting them for names and dates but, like so many of these graveyards, the less modern of the memorials were all smothered in long grass. Lots of neglected stones had fallen to the ground and were overgrown while others were tilted at alarming angles.

Some parts of the graveyard, deserted by modern grave-tenders, were seriously overgrown, so much so that those corners looked like unexplored wasteland.

And so Claude found himself once again hacking away at the growth with the tip of his scythe, cutting away the tough old grass so that he could read the entire inscription. In some cases, the inscriptions continued to the very base of the gravestone and he began to think his task was going to be unproductive. Stone after stone received his treatment, but none revealed what he sought.

He spent nearly two hours at Stovensby without success and said, "Come on, Alfred. Off we go again. Thackerston next . . ."

* * *

At Ashfordly Police Station, the telephone was ringing in Sergeant Blaketon's office. He snatched at it, hoping that it wasn't another vicar or churchwarden ringing to report a theft. But it wasn't; it was Inspector Murchison.

"This afternoon's football match, Sergeant," she began. "I take it you have selected your finest officers? We need to put on a good show, you know, we need to keep the peace in a friendly but very positive manner."

"I have selected the cream of Ashfordly section, ma'am," said Blaketon. "The very best."

"Good, because I have received some advance intelligence from Durham County Constabulary. We have learned that six bus loads of fans from Crook are heading down the Great North Road, intent on the match this afternoon in Whitby."

"Six bus loads of crooks, ma'am?" Blaketon was determined to take a rise out of this woman; he disliked women inspectors, especially when they were younger than him and more especially when they had fewer years of service in the Force.

"Not six bus loads of crooks, Sergeant! I wish you would listen carefully! Six bus loads of football fans from Crook. Now, I want no trouble in Whitby, no fighting . . ."

"I'm sure my officers will cope, ma'am, we will segregate the crooks from the home team fans."

"They're not crooks, Sergeant!"

"Crook fans," he grinned to himself. "We will separate the Crook fans from the Whitby Town supporters. That should prevent any riots or mayhem."

"Good. Now, there have been two more reports of offertory box break-ins this morning, Sergeant. Not in Ashfordly section, I grant you, but close enough to your boundary to be the work of the same person. This is not good enough, this man is making fools of us, so I want every effort to catch the thief . . ."

"But my best men will be at the football ground this afternoon."

"That's all, Sergeant," and she replaced the telephone.

Later that morning, PC Alf Ventress arrived for duty. He was carrying a knapsack over his shoulder and was smartly dressed in his best uniform, his shoulders surprisingly free of cigarette ash. As Alf waited, Sergeant Blaketon came through from his office.

"Ventress!" he boomed. "What's this? We're not going on holiday, you know."

"It's my refreshments, Sergeant, in case we're late back."

"Refreshments? We're going to Whitby, not Wembley, we'll be back by teatime."

"You never know, serge. Anything can happen in Whitby. Be prepared, that's my motto."

"Right, well, we'd best be off. We've Rowan to collect at Aidensfield and I hope that inspector's in a better mood this afternoon. She's fretting about public disorder, she's been told there's six bus loads of Crook supporters coming to the match."

"I'm sure we can cope, Sergeant," said Alf Ventress with confidence.

As they were about to leave, Phil Bellamy entered the office; he was casually dressed in civilian clothes, but sported a blue and white scarf around his neck. He was carrying a holdall and a pair of football boots.

"Up the Blues!" he grinned at Blaketon.

Sergeant Blaketon looked him up and down, then said, "I hope you're not expecting a lift in an official vehicle while you're dressed like that, Bellamy!"

"No, serge, I've got my own transport organised. It's picking me up in ten minutes, but I've got some entries I hadn't time to make yesterday, in the "Visits to Licensed Premises" register," and Phil placed his bag on the floor, unzipped it and pulled out a sheet of paper. "I thought I'd best get them entered before I forgot."

"You'd be too busy thinking about football, if I know you!" retorted Blaketon. "Football instead of police work! Well, get your entries made before you forget them altogether, and next time remember to do your administrative duties on time, at the time!"

"Yes, Sergeant."

"Right, we'll leave you to get on, then," said Blaketon. "We're off to collect Rowan and then we'll see you at Whitby. And mind you're not late for the match! I don't want one of my constables being late for his own kick-off!"

"Serge!" smiled Bellamy.

"Oh, and Bellamy?"

"Serge?"

"Mind you score! I want a win, you know, no second best when an Ashfordly section man is centre forward!"

"I'll score, serge, you'll see."

And so, leaving Phil to lock the office when he'd made his entries, Sergeant Blaketon and PC Ventress departed, with Blaketon at the wheel of the highly polished official car. When he was satisfied they had left the premises, Phil delved into his holdall and pulled out a gaily wrapped parcel and a birthday card in a crisp white envelope. He hurried into Blaketon's office and placed the gift and the card upon his desk, then pulled a piece of paper from a drawer. With a black pen, he wrote upon it in large lettering: "Happy Birthday, serge, from the lads."

With a piece of sticky tape, he stuck this on Blaketon's office notice board, stood back to admire his work, and then left. Locking the office with his own key, Phil walked into town to await his lift to the football ground.

He was pleased his colleagues had been selected for duties at the ground — at least Blaketon would see him play and that thought gave Phil a sense of pride. He'd play his heart out this afternoon, he'd put on a real good show for his pals from Ashfordly section.

While Phil was awaiting his lift, Sergeant Blaketon was easing to a halt outside the police house, Aidensfield. It was precisely one o'clock and so he pipped the horn.

"I hope Rowan isn't going to keep us waiting, Ventress. I don't want the new inspector to think we're slack timekeepers at Ashfordly!"

"He's coming, serge," said Alf who was dying for a smoke, but he knew better than to light-up in Blaketon's immaculate car. He might find a quiet corner somewhere during the match, one of the toilets maybe, or some other sheltered place where he could have a puff at his cigarettes.

Nick, in his best uniform, which was all pressed and clean, hurried across to the waiting car and climbed into the rear seat. "Good afternoon, Sergeant, Alf," he smiled at them. "You were nearly late then, Rowan!" grumbled Blaketon. "Or nearly early, depending on which way you look at it, serge," chuckled Nick as he settled down. "But we'll be in Whitby in good time, well before two o'clock."

"So long as that inspector doesn't get a chance to have a go at us . . . you know, I'd be far happier staying in Ashfordly, trying to catch that offertory box thief!"

"Oh, I don't know about that, serge," said Alf. "I do love a good football match, and it'll do us good, getting out of a rut like this."

"A rut, Ventress? I don't regard the policing of Ashfordly as being in a rut! As the officer in charge, I regard it as a major responsibility, far better than wasting time at seaside football matches," and the car set off.

"Oh, I do like to be beside the seaside," sang Nick from the rear seat, at which Alf joined in. Soon, they were singing together in a very tuneless way, the familiar strains of "I do like to be beside the seaside, Oh, I do like to be beside the sea. Oh I do like to walk along the prom, prom, prom, tiddly aye, tiddly aye, tiddly pom, pom, pom!"

"Shut up, you noisy shower," bellowed Blaketon. "I can't hear myself think above that racket and besides, I can't hear the official radio. We might just get a check call from the new inspector and if she hears that racket. We *are* on duty, you know. Ashfordly section at its finest! You make me wonder what the worst would be like!"

They lapsed into silence as Sergeant Blaketon guided them across the wild expanse of the North York Moors and across the picturesque summit of Blue Bank above Sleights with its expansive views towards the coast. Nick never ceased to admire the splendid panorama as they continued their way to Whitby Town's cliff-top football ground. When they arrived, Inspector Murchison, forbidding and unsmiling, was waiting.

She stood outside the high fence which surrounded the ground, hands behind her back and feet apart, as she watched the shining car ease to a halt at the kerbside. Sergeant Blaketon, muttering to his crew "Best behaviour, you lot!" put on his cap, brushed flecks of imaginary dust from his uniform with his hands, and then climbed out. He flung up a smart salute as he said, "Ashfordly contingent present and correct, ma'am!"

Nick and Alf followed suit, each saluting the stolid figure of the woman inspector. She looked at her watch.

"Nice timing, Sergeant," she said. "You're ten minutes early. But I'll brief you all now. No time like the present, eh? So, line up against this fence."

They obeyed and shuffled into position, like a guard of honour at a national monument. As they were preparing for her inspection, small groups of Whitby Town supporters were heading for the entrance and shouting "Up the Blues" as they waved their blue and white scarves. But Inspector Murchison ignored their presence as she said, "Right, Sergeant Blaketon and the Ashfordly contingent, these are your duties. I want no fighting, no litter, no swearing in a public place, no drinking alcohol in the street, no undue noise . . ."

Alf Ventress grinned.

"Are you referring to us or the public, ma'am?"

"And I want no frivolity from police officers on duty, PC Ventress!" was her cutting response. "We want no complaints from the public, especially those who live near the ground, and I want no grumbles about our service to the public. In every respect, gentlemen, this will be an orderly football match."

She paused and looked at each in turn, daring them to contradict or disobey her.

"Now," she said. "Your duties. You are all on street car parking and bus parking duties. Streets are allocated for parking. This is one such street and I want you to ensure that all vehicles are correctly parked and that there is no obstruction to other traffic."

Alf Ventress spoke again. "Does this mean we won't see the match, ma'am? We can't, if we're outside the ground."

"That's right, PC Ventress. You are on duty outside the ground, and sergeant?"

"Ma'am?" replied Blaketon.

"You are in charge of these officers, outside the ground."

Sergeant Blaketon was resigned to this and simply said, "Yes, ma'am, whatever you say. So where will you be, should I need to contact you?"

"I shall be inside the ground, Sergeant, for most of the time, that is. I may also tour the streets, just as a precaution you understand, to make sure things are going smoothly. But I do enjoy a good football match, Sergeant."

And with that, she walked away. Blaketon did not see the quiet smile of success on her face.

CHAPTER VIII

For the Ashfordly contingent of police officers, the football match between Crook and Whitby Town was extremely boring, even if it was a cup tie. Sergeant Blaketon, Alf Ventress and Nick had parked all their coaches and cars in the designated streets without any problems and the fans were all inside the ground, now the responsibility of other officers.

There was nothing to do until the fans began to disperse after the match but even so, Blaketon's men had not been allowed into the ground. From their position outside, they could see nothing of the game. A high wooden fence, without any viewing holes, stood between them and the match and their only indication of progress was the noise of the crowd. But even that was not very informative. No one emerged from the ground to update them on progress, and the shouts and cheers gave no indication of the strength of either team.

The only knowledge they had was that, by half-time, neither side had scored. That gem of information came from a newspaper seller who was leaving to collect a further supply of *Evening Gazettes* for sale to the crowd as they departed.

It was while hanging about, getting progressively more bored with the inactivity, that Nick realised Alf had vanished. Somehow, he had just faded from the scene — Nick guessed he'd slipped away for a crafty smoke somewhere, or a cup of tea.

Apparently, Sergeant Blaketon hadn't noticed Alf's disappearing trick, so, to protect Alf wherever he was, Nick tried to keep the sergeant engaged in conversation.

"I wonder how Phil's playing?" he tried to think of something sensible to say to the sergeant.

"Not very well, Rowan, if the score's anything to go by," retorted Sergeant Blaketon. "It's not a very stimulating game if you ask me!"

"Well, it's still nil-nil," observed Nick. "So Phil's teammates are containing Crook. They haven't lost yet, so Phil must be doing something worthwhile."

"He's either chasing balls or chasing women," mused Blaketon. "His mind should be on higher things, Rowan, like swotting for his promotion exam or studying criminology."

"Give him time, serge, he's not worried about his career prospects just yet."

"I hope you're thinking of promotion, Rowan, it's not much fun being a constable all through your career, you've always got too many people telling you what to do. You need to get a step on the ladder of success, Rowan, think of your self-esteem, your career, aim for two pips on your shoulder or a splash of scrambled egg around the peak of your cap."

"Yes, Sergeant," smiled Nick. "I don't aim to be a constable all my life."

"So do your job to the best of your ability and don't get into trouble, Rowan. Which reminds me, my enquiries around Ashfordly show that your wife recently bought a screwdriver. From the ironmongers. A large screwdriver, Rowan."

"That's right, serge, with a three-eighths blade. I needed it to do some work on my MG, there was a stubborn screw in a bracket that had to come off."

"And you ride a motorcycle, Rowan?"

"I do, serge." Nick was puzzled by Blaketon's sudden switch of conversation. What had all this to do with promotion examinations and career prospects?

Blaketon pursed his lips and looked steadily at Nick.

"I am thinking of good policemen, Rowan, policemen who would never commit a breach of the police regulations, let alone commit a crime."

"A crime, Sergeant?"

"I am thinking of those offertory box thefts, Rowan. The suspect uses a three-eighths screwdriver and arrives at the scene on a motorcycle, by all accounts . . ."

"Sergeant! God! You don't suspect me, do you? I mean, I'm not a criminal, serge . . . I mean . . . well, Kate didn't get that screwdriver till yesterday anyway, those boxes have been raided over the past few weeks."

"I know, Rowan, I'm not for one moment suggesting you are a criminal, nor am I suggesting that you have been raiding those boxes. But, like lots of other people, I have been examining the evidence and the evidence does show that the raider is a person with a three-eighths screwdriver and a motorbike. If you see what I mean!"

"But surely people don't suspect me, serge?" Nick was horrified at the thought.

"No, but I think it might be in your own interest to find out who else has got such a screwdriver, and rides a motor-cycle, don't you?"

"I see what you mean, serge."

"And Inspector Murchison is putting pressure on to get these crimes detected, Rowan! Need I say more?"

"You had me worried then, serge!" breathed Nick.

"And now I intend to get Ventress worried. Where is he, Rowan? He's skiving somewhere, I'll bet, he'll have sneaked away to have a crafty drag at those ghastly cigarettes of his. They smell like old socks, Rowan, and old socks worn by very old policemen on very old beats in very old boots."

Nick glanced around but could see no sign of Alf.

"Sorry, serge, but I've no idea where he is."

Blaketon began to stroll along the line of cars which were now parked along the street. Midway along, almost hidden by the other vehicles, was Blaketon's official car and there, seated in the rear, was the contented Alf Ventress. He had his knapsack on his knee and a teacloth spread across his uniform trousers as he was preparing to enjoy a snack.

A flask of tea stood on the floor; it was already opened and Alf had a pair of hard-boiled eggs in his hands. One was in each fist and he was about to crack them together to break the shells when Blaketon opened the door and poked his head inside.

"Don't you dare, Ventress!" he bellowed. "Not in my clean car . . . you are supposed to be on duty, not using my highly polished, dirt free, non-smoking official motor car as a mobile canteen!"

"But there's nothing to do, serge! We've done the parking, those cars and buses will get away without us worrying about them."

"We are here because Inspector Murchison has ordered us to be here, Ventress. Orders are orders. We are not paid to think, that's the job of somebody else. Now, get out of my car, clean up that mess, and get back to your post."

Alf looked at the two eggs.

"Serge, we should be going home, we're wasting time here."

"Ventress, orders are orders. Out. Now!"

"If you say so, Sergeant," and Alf reluctantly replaced the eggs, put the lid back on his flask and returned everything to the knapsack. Then he clambered out and put on his helmet. As Blaketon walked back to his original position near the tall fence, he said, "Ventress, you are the senior constable in Ashfordly section and so, to stop your boredom, I'm going to give you some responsibility."

"Really, Sergeant?" Alf looked puzzled.

"I am going to undertake a short supervisory patrol of the neighbouring streets, Ventress, to check on parking in readiness for the outflow of vehicles. I am going to leave you in charge of this stretch of the road. You may now rejoin PC Rowan."

"Oh, very good, Sergeant."

And as Alf continued forward to rejoin Nick for a further period of inactivity, Sergeant Blaketon veered away and marched steadfastly towards the town centre.

"Where's he going?" asked Nick.

"Search me," Alf shrugged his shoulders. "He said he was going on a supervisory patrol!"

"I'll bet he's going for a cup of tea himself!" grinned Nick. "Crafty old beggar!"

With Blaketon out of the way, Alf decided he would make a recce of the vicinity in the hope there might be somewhere for a smoke or some means of viewing the second half of the match. As he wandered along the fence, he turned across a portion of waste ground with a rough lane running along it; the fence followed the lane for a hundred yards or so and finally, as he walked along, he found a missing plank. It left a gap in the fence — and it provided a wonderful view of the pitch.

"Nick!" he called. "Hey, come here. We can watch the match . . . I'll get my flask and sandwiches, we can share the grub while we keep out of the public view . . ."

"Right!"

And so, in the absence of their strict master, the two constables settled down to watch the final part of the game, each nourished by a hard-boiled egg, a ham sandwich and a share of the hot sweet tea from Alf's flask.

"Phil's playing well," observed Alf. "He's running rings round those Crook defenders . . . I reckon they've run themselves out of steam and Whitby'll beat them . . . this is a good match, eh?"

"Good old Phil," breathed Nick. "If he scores, it'll make my day — especially if we see him do it!"

* * *

For Sergeant Blaketon, the fact that he was working in a town like Whitby for however short a period, presented an opportunity to search for some second-hand books. He had a large selection of popular novels by people like Dickens, Trollope, Hardy and Walpole, but his pride was his collection of Bronte editions. He had at least one copy of every edition of every Bronte novel, some in rather poor condition, and so his quest for finer specimens was never-ending. He wanted to own the best collection in England, he wanted to rival even the Bronte Society itself.

Oscar Blaketon knew there was a small but very highly regarded second-hand bookshop in Silver Street, Whitby and this afternoon's duty, with its long moments of inactivity, offered an ideal opportunity to visit the shop.

He realised, of course, that such private expeditions were no part of a police officer's duty but, he had reasoned, all the town's officers were on duty at the match. This meant he could undertake what he called a supervisory patrol of the streets which also meant that if he just happened to be passing the shop during that patrol, then he might be tempted to pop in.

In leaving Ventress and Rowan alone, he knew they would find something to occupy them and so it was that Sergeant Oscar Blaketon happened to be walking past the second-hand book shop. The door was standing open, almost tempting him to enter. He paused to glance at the window, his trained eyes scanning the display, and then he looked up and down the street. There was no one about; Silver Street was off the beaten track anyway, but at this precise moment, it was deserted. There was not a person in sight and so, like a wraith, he disappeared into the book shop.

He moved among the shelves, all packed with a variety of desirable volumes; he passed the local history section, the transport section, the war section, the natural history shelf, the travel shelf . . . and then he found the fiction section with its array of novels by Britain's foremost authors.

Blaketon owned copies of most of the books on display but as he was seeking anything by one of the Bronte sisters, he heard a voice behind.

"Good afternoon, Sergeant," it was a small man with spectacles. "Can I help you?"

"Oh, yes," Blaketon was partly taken by surprise because he hadn't heard the man's approach. "I was just passing the shop and thought I'd pop in — I collect Bronte novels, you see, all editions."

"Ah, well, I'm sorry. I've just sold my only copy — *Wuthering Heights* it was. I took it into stock only yesterday, put it on the shelf this morning and it went before lunch. A lady bought it, an early Blackamoor edition."

Blaketon smiled his disappointment. "I'd have liked that. Oh, well, that's the way it goes. But I might be back."

"You're new to the town, Sergeant?" the man commented. "I'm from Ashfordly," Blaketon told him. "Our boundaries have been altered slightly, and from time to time in the future, I might be doing duty in Whitby, like today. So I shall make a point of coming into your shop."

"Well, I do get Bronte editions in quite frequently, sometimes in sets and sometimes individual volumes. I could always drop you a line if you're a very keen collector."

"Sergeant O. Blaketon, Ashfordly Police Station will find me," said Oscar. "I'd appreciate that."

And as he turned to leave, he was horrified to see the distinctive figure of Inspector Murchison passing the doorway of this very shop. She glanced inside as she passed and Blaketon tried to conceal himself behind some bookcases.

Had she seen him? He waited until he reckoned she'd gone.

The shopkeeper was saying, "I could always place your name on our search list, Sergeant, and if a dealer has a rare Bronte title, you would be informed before it was put on general sale . . ."

"Oh, er, right," he wasn't really concentrating on the man's words any longer. "Yes, that would be nice. Thank you. Well, I must be moving along, the football crowds will soon be turning out!"

"It's quite a walk to the ground, Sergeant," smiled the shopkeeper, but as Blaketon moved towards the door, Inspector Murchison came in.

"I thought I saw you in here, Sergeant, when I came past just now," she said pointedly. "I trust things are in order at the football ground?"

"Er, I was just familiarising myself with the town, ma'am," he said. "I've left my men in control at the football ground. I have complete faith in them, they're the cream of Ashfordly section, totally reliable. They can work without close supervision, I assure you!"

"Let us hope so, Sergeant. Now, shall we walk back to the football ground together? Back to where you should be on duty?" she added pointedly.

And so, marching side by side in precise military fashion, Sergeant Blaketon and Inspector Murchison strode through the streets as they made for Whitby football ground.

As they approached it about quarter of an hour later, there was no sign of Ventress or Rowan on the street where he had left them. Poor old Oscar began to fear the worst . . . they'd let him down, and just when the inspector was going to discover their lapse! They drew nearer to the ground with Blaketon desperately looking for his officers; he saw the high fence come into view along the street which contained the rows of parked cars, and then he saw his men. His heart sank; they were peering through a hole in the fence! Had she seen them?

Blaketon tried to ignore the sight because it consisted of two uniformed police officers, with their helmets on the backs of their heads, as they stooped to peer through a hole in the railings. And both were cheering and shouting. Worse still, Ventress was puffing at a cigarette and at that moment, the crowd roared in excitement and shouted "Goal, goal!"

"Phil scored!" shouted Nick as he jumped up and punched the air with his fist. "What a goal! He beat that goalie as if he wasn't there . . . great stuff . . . !"

Blaketon realised that Inspector Murchison had seen the display and decided to act.

"Ventress, Rowan!" he bellowed. "Get back to your posts this minute! This is disgraceful . . ."

They turned and saw the two senior officers bearing down on them. Alf nipped his cigarette and stuffed it into his pocket as Nick replaced his helmet and strode back to the street, with Alf following.

They heard Inspector Murchison saying, "Your men work very well without supervision, you told me, Sergeant Blaketon. The best of Ashfordly section, you said. I'd say they were neglecting their duty, I'd say they were improperly dressed and at least one of them was smoking on duty, Sergeant. I shall expect you to deal with them accordingly, Sergeant!" And off she marched, heading for the entrance to the ground as Blaketon came towards them, red-faced and wishing a hole would open up beneath him.

"I shall speak to you two when we return to Ashfordly," was all he said. "Now get back on patrol, both of you!"

"Sorry, Sergeant," they said meekly.

CHAPTER IX

While the football match was in progress at Whitby that Saturday afternoon, several members of the Killing Pits Club had assembled on the moor at the outskirts of Aidensfield. There were fewer than last night, perhaps five or six cars and up to a dozen members comprising youths and girls. Indeed two of the members had gone to the football match, being keen supporters of Whitby Town, but the others had assembled for a Saturday afternoon outing of some kind. This gathering was to enable a decision to be made. Should they drive out to York, or the coast or visit a ruined abbey?

As they were assembling, someone noticed an old Austin A40 coming down the hill towards them and at the wheel was Graham Blaketon. Beside him was his pal, Denis Myers, and the car sported "L" plates to the front and rear.

As he drove, Graham noticed the gathering of youngsters and, turning to Denis, asked, "Shall we stop and see what they're up to?"

"Sure," agreed Denis, although he was not too anxious to join the club members; after all, they had rejected his pleas for membership so there was no real point in trying again. But he knew Graham was friendly with some of them, old school friends mainly. Graham turned his car towards the group of vehicles, drove it onto the smooth grass and stopped.

He and Denis climbed out just as a small motorcycle chugged to a halt beside them. The rider turned off his engine and sat astride the machine to speak to them. It was Gordon Turnbull.

"Hey, what's happened to you, Gordon?" laughed one of the group. "Got sick of driving around in posh cars, have you?"

"My radiator's sprung a leak, so I can't use the car until I get it fixed," he explained. "It's a huge hole, I can't go more than a couple of miles before it's drained dry. I thought I might have a ride over to Ponderosa Scrap Yard to see if I can find a good second-hand radiator, then I saw this lot gathering and thought I'd stop to say hello." Then he turned to Graham and smiled, "So what are you and our Denis doing here?"

"I saw the group," Graham told Gordon. "Me and Denis were off to Scarborough then I saw them all here so we stopped for a chat. We wondered if there was going to be a club outing somewhere, Scarborough maybe?"

"Aren't they doing the run this afternoon?" asked Gordon, directing his question to anyone who might answer.

"I've no idea," Denis responded. "I've not heard anybody talk about it. I mean, I haven't really had chance to find out yet, we've only just got here."

"Graham," smiled Gordon with just a hint of cunning in his eyes as he changed the subject. "They tell me your dad's on duty at Whitby this afternoon?"

"That's right, Whitby Town's playing Crook, they were expecting a big crowd. Rowan's gone from Aidensfield as well, and Ventress from Ashfordly."

"So there'll be no local coppers to worry us if we did a run this afternoon?" beamed Gordon. "A daylight one. Now that would be a good idea, a real test! It'd be far better than a night-time trial."

Denis shrugged his shoulders. Such an idea held no appeal to him because he wouldn't be allowed to participate, and Graham was not too happy with the idea. The idea of youths racing around the moors on a Saturday afternoon, when the roads could be busy with tourists and local people, was not one which commended itself to him. He experienced a sense of foreboding; a shudder ran down his spine, but he said nothing. He had no wish to be regarded as a spoil-sport, nor to give anyone the opportunity of suggesting he was behaving like his father! He knew most of the lads were extremely good drivers and nothing had happened yet. None had had an accident, and the police had never stopped them — the only complaint was about a bit of noise and that was not serious. Noise never hurt anybody.

As they had been talking, three more cars arrived, their drivers having seen the somewhat impromptu gathering of the club. There were girls too. Whatever the members decided, it looked like being an exciting Saturday afternoon's entertainment.

Gordon was now enthusing over the idea.

"I reckon somebody could beat five minutes fifty-five seconds this afternoon," he was saying. "It's perfect. The roads are dry, the weather's fine, visibility's good, there's no strong winds. So let's go for a record, shall we? Best time out of three circuits each? How about that?"

Before Graham could add his reservations to that idea, Gordon whistled through his fingers to attract the attention of the few who had gathered. He hoisted his motorcycle onto its rest and left it as he strode to a slightly higher piece of moorland.

"Right," he said, having gained their attention. "How about a record attempt this afternoon?"

He went on to explain about the absence of police officers, and the fact that conditions were ideal for a very fast time. A persuasive speaker, Gordon had no difficulty convincing them it was a good idea. What had started as a gathering of club members for little more than a chat and a comparison of vehicles, had suddenly developed into the beginning of a serious contest.

"Right," he said. "We need to get things organised. Three circuits, the fastest time counting. That gives you three chances to make a name for yourself. We need a time-keeper and a half-way marshal. Graham," he turned to young Blaketon. "How about you being the half-way marshal? They've all got to pass you to qualify — that stops them taking short cuts; you clock their times as they pass you."

"Sure," agreed Graham Blaketon, if a little reluctantly.

"You remember the half-way point?"

"You bet!" Graham tried to show some enthusiasm. "Bracken Corner. I once fell off my push bike there, when we were doing a teenage kids' race!"

"That's the place. Look, can you take Denis' dad's car? We can give you five minutes to get there and set up for your timing stint."

"There's nowhere to park a car there, Gordon, it's a very narrow road. I'll need a lift out there. Maybe somebody could take me out there and come back for the trial?"

Gordon didn't reply to that suggestion but suddenly flashed a smile and said, "Tell you what, you could take my motorbike. You've passed your test for bikes, haven't you?"

"Sure, and cars."

"Right, there'll be no problem parking the bike, so take that. And I have a job for our Denis. Right, off you go, settle yourself in at Bracken Corner and we'll set them off in ten minutes time. One-minute intervals as usual."

"Synchronise watches first!" said Graham, and so he and Gordon made sure each watch showed exactly the same time. Then Gordon whistled again and shouted, "Right, Graham's off to be half-way marshal. We start in ten minutes. Now, I'm feeling generous so tonight, I'll buy drinks all night for the crew of the car that's fastest at the half-way stage."

This announcement was greeted with cheers and whistles, as Gordon continued, "But, as usual, the slowest round the circuit pays for the first round as before . . . how about that?"

They all indicated their agreement and then Gordon asked one of the girls to write every driver's name on a piece of paper.

There would be a draw for the order of starting and as these arrangements were being finalised, Graham mounted the small motorbike, kicked it into life and set off through Aidensfield.

He enjoyed the feel of the wind through his hair, this being long before the compulsory wearing of crash helmets, as he guided the tough little machine around the lanes. There was a series of steep hills and sharp corners before he arrived at the place known as Bracken Corner. It was a steep, winding hill between elevated pieces of moorland, almost like a gorge in fact, and once the cars had passed through here, they could complete the circuit without cheating by local short cut. He found a flat area to park the machine then climbed onto his vantage point to await the first competitor.

As Graham was going about his responsibilities, Gordon approached Denis.

"Now then our Denis," he began, using the term Denis' mother always used when she spoke about him. "What have we got lined up for you, eh?"

"Starter, I should think," muttered Denis. "I've got a white handkerchief, and a watch."

And at that point, he experienced a sudden attack of dizziness. It was only slight, but he felt the world begin to spin around him and he rested one hand against the car to steady himself.

"You all right, our Denis?" asked Gordon with mock concern.

"Yeh, nothing. Just lost my balance, I'm OK now."

"Well, I had a nice thought, our Denis," oozed Gordon. "I mean, you've been asking us for ages if the club would accept you and we can't. Rules, you know. You have to be a car owner and driver, as you know."

Denis looked at Gordon, wondering what was coming next.

"Well," continued Gordon. "This event's a bit special and it is Saturday afternoon, I'm feeling in a happy and generous mood, the police are miles away and you have a car, right there beside you!"

"It's my dad's," muttered Denis, his head still reeling from his attack of dizziness.

"And you're a learner. But I thought I might persuade the others to let you have a go this afternoon. You know, do the circuit, as a sort of test."

"Test?" asked Denis.

"Well, we know how keen you are to join us, and you have always been a member in the past, with your pedal bike and motorbike, and so I thought that if you could do the circuit in less than, say six minutes, then we might accept you."

"In Dad's car, you mean?"

"Why not? The cops are away from the area, you could take the "L" plates off and who would know? You're a good driver and all you have to do is get that old crate around the course in less than six minutes. A doddle, I'd say. And if you did, we'd accept you as a special member, even without owning a car. How about that?"

"Well, I'm not sure . . . I mean, it's an old car, to get round in less than six minutes, well, you really have to be motoring and besides, I am a learner . . ."

"You'll never get another chance like this, Denis. I'll bet your mum will never let you have the car again, it's only because Graham's here that you've got it . . ."

Denis knew they were right. His mother could not drive and there'd be precious few other opportunities. It took only a moment's thought for him to agree.

Gordon smiled; Gordon knew the old car would never get around the circuit within six minutes, but he did enjoy seeing poor old Denis suffer . . . the fellow had no money, no style, no girlfriend . . .

Having secured Denis' consent, Gordon whistled for attention and put the proposal to the other club members. It was very simple — if Denis, in his dad's old car, could complete the circuit within six minutes this afternoon, then the club would accept him as a special member. The others, listening to Gordon's suggestion, all agreed.

And so Denis Myers, unwell, dizzy and very much a learner driver, found himself agreeing to perform the Killing Pits circuit at a speed which would test even the most powerful of sports cars.

Denis, wondering what on earth he had let himself in for, moved around to the front of his father's car. He began to untie the "L" plate which was tied to the bumper bar but as he stooped, he felt another attack of giddiness. He placed a hand on the bonnet to steady himself, hoping no one had seen his unsteadiness.

"This is going to be a great day for the club," beamed Gordon. "And as I haven't got a car today, I'll be timekeeper."

CHAPTER X

As Graham Blaketon was endeavouring to establish himself in the best viewing position at Bracken Corner, so his mother was on her way to Aidensfield from Whitby. In her smart, clean car she was driving very carefully, slowly even, because she was admiring the stunning and seemingly endless views across the dramatic windswept moors.

Acre upon acre of heather was spread before her like a huge coverlet and in the far distance, almost shrouded with mist, were the deep dales which contained pretty villages. Almost treeless, these heights were beautiful in the summer and spring, extraordinarily beautiful in the autumn when the ling was in bloom but terrifying in the depths of winter when the snow could obliterate everything. It could isolate villages for weeks on end, it could smother the sheep which roamed these heights and it could fill the rivers with flood water when it melted.

But today, in the middle of March, the day was crisp and clear. The sky, with small white clouds hugging the far horizon, was a delightful pale blue as the afternoon sun bathed the entire landscape in a healthy pale glow. As she drove, Joan could see in the distance on the hill, the three white radomes of Fylingdale Ballistic Missile Early Warning Station.

Like a clutch of giant duck eggs, they rose from the heather, in the manner of a curiously attractive surrealistic sculpture. In the foreground were the sturdy cottages of Aidensfield, a village which nestled in a green hollow surrounded by mile after mile of open and wild moorland. The squat tower of the parish church rose above the houses which were constructed of solid grey moorland stone with blue slates. They were huddled together as the sheep huddled together to protect themselves against the ravages of the harsh moorland weather. She could see the narrow winding road which led from the main highway, dipping and weaving across the heights, vanishing into a deep dale before rising at the far side to cross a lofty ridge. Down there, Joan realised, people were working and resting, enjoying their gardens, going for walks, having fun. It was a far, far cry from the dusty and noisy life of a city and even a far cry from her own suburban world of semi-detached houses and neat lawns in the market town of Pickering.

As Joan drove along, absorbed with her thoughts, she came to understand why Oscar was quite content to remain on these moors. He had never sought promotion, never had any desire to work or live in a larger town. He much preferred the friendliness of Ashfordly. A busy market town, it was smaller than Pickering although it was a market town in its own right, with its own market square, old cottages with red pantile roofs and even a peer of the realm in the big house.

He owned most of the properties in Ashfordly, but the town offered an enviable kind of peace, a homely life style, a community which looked upon itself as a large village. And Oscar Blaketon was in charge of the policing of that town — that was something he loved. He was king of his own territory, master of his own destiny, a man of some substance. No wonder he'd never wanted promotion, no wonder he'd never wanted to be transferred to a larger police station. She smiled at her own thoughts. There were times she'd bullied him, tried to make him leave the area for a more vibrant place, but he'd always refused.

Joan realised he still loved her. In some ways, that hurt. He'd never been one for revealing his true feelings but he'd been devastated by the divorce. He had seen himself as a loving father and husband, working hard to maintain his wife and small son while she'd seen him as a tireless police sergeant who was always at work with no time for her or their son. He'd spent all his life in uniform, working in his office far longer than he need, always checking on his men, worrying about his bosses and making sure the public did not break the law, even when he was off duty.

Dear old Oscar, she thought. So conscientious, so diligent but oh, so boring! If only he'd taken the occasional evening off to visit the theatre or the cinema or a restaurant together . . . if only. But it was all over now.

She liked him; there was never a question of hatred in her decision to leave him and at the time of the divorce, there was no other man. It was simply that their marriage was over. She'd always been faithful to Oscar and she knew he'd been faithful to her — he was still faithful to her. He'd never found another woman. Even after the divorce, he'd never turned to a woman for friendship or comfort but had steadfastly lived alone, absorbing himself in his work and never complaining. She knew all this from friends whose husbands were still serving and sometimes, she wondered if she'd really been true to dear old Oscar. But if she had remained married to him, her life would have been so boring, so unfulfilled . . .

After the divorce, she'd met Bruce Forrester; they'd married and had been very happy until his unexpected death last year. A heart attack, a sudden death at the early age of fifty. So now she was alone again — except that Graham was living with her, at least until he completed his education and found a job.

It was nice, therefore, to have bought Oscar something for his birthday, especially something he would cherish. His birthday was tomorrow, Sunday, and today she was driving back into Aidensfield, a slight diversion from her return journey to Pickering. She'd promised to leave the joint present at the Myers' house for Graham to deliver. Graham had arranged to see his father and he would deliver the present along with his own card. Joan found herself beginning to sing.

With the gorgeous spread of the moors ahead of her, she started to sing Engelbert Humperdinck's *Last Waltz* as she turned down a narrow lane signposted "Aidensfield". She knew she would have to drive carefully along this lane because it was extremely narrow in places with sharp corners and steep inclines. Some of these hills had gradients of 1-in-3 and in some places, it was impossible to pass another car. You had to reverse to special passing places, so great care was needed.

She reduced her speed by a fraction.

* * *

Denis was drawn No. 5. Seated nervously at the wheel of his father's old A40 with the "L" plates hidden beneath the seat, Denis awaited his turn. Gordon, using a yellow duster as a starting flag, had waved off No. 4 and so Denis eased his car forward to the starting point.

"Half a minute to go, our Denis," shouted Gordon. "Get your revs up!"

Denis settled into the seat and depressed the accelerator to rev the tired old engine but as he moved, another attack of giddiness and nausea began to sweep over him. No one seemed to notice. He took a deep breath and closed his eyes, feeling the engine revving and hearing the activity around him. He really ought to withdraw, he decided; he wasn't fit to drive let alone race through the lanes. But a girl, Lucy Benson, tapped on the window and said, "Good luck, Denis, you can do it!"

He smiled at her. She was nice, was Lucy. Maybe in the pub tonight, if he beat the time limit now, he could buy her a drink and talk to her . . . she was obviously keen for him to succeed. So yes, he would beat six minutes! He would get around the course in less than six minutes, he would show he was as good as the others, he would become a member of the Killing Pits Club and then he'd get a car and a girl like Lucy!

"Fifteen seconds," called Gordon Turnbull, raising his yellow duster above his head and not looking at the worried Denis. Denis engaged first gear, keeping the clutch depressed as the countdown began.

"Ten, nine, eight, seven . . . Ready, our Denis . . . five, four, three, two, one. Go! Go! Go! Give it some welly."

And so, with the engine revving at its limit, Denis Myers tore away from the grassy edge of the moor and the old car hurtled along the village street of Aidensfield. Out of first gear, into second, more revs, more acceleration, a racing change into third . . . watch that silly ewe and twin lambs . . . a woman with a little girl . . . now top. Nearly missed top . . . it grated . . . got it. Ooops, a dizzy spell again . . . ignore it . . . keep going, keep that speedo needle on sixty . . .

And Denis was racing through Aidensfield towards the distant moor as the speedometer flickered around the sixty miles an hour mark. The road was deserted, there was good visibility, the surface was dry . . . and he found he was enjoying the experience.

He wasn't dizzy any more as he pressed the accelerator just a little further to the floorboards.

* * *

Graham Blaketon was standing on an elevated portion of moorland. Below him was the steep twisting road; it came down from the heights at each side of him, from left to right, dropping into a dip in the road with a sharp corner at the very bottom. Narrow, deep and blind, the corner was treacherous. From his vantage point, he could see both ways but from the bottom of the dip, from the actual road itself, you could see nothing. Even for drivers who were familiar with the road, it was the sort of corner you had to crawl around just in case something was coming the other way.

For young men driving to the limit, this was the most testing stretch of the circuit. By slowing down to a speed which was necessary to take the corner in safety, precious seconds were lost but by taking the corner at speed, danger was created. The best way of negotiating that corner in a car rested with individual drivers, based on the prevailing conditions — even on a motorcycle, it was difficult.

Anything might be coming in the opposite direction — another car, a motorcycle, a pedal cyclist, a band of hikers, a single moorland sheep or a flock of them, a dog, Arnold Merryweather's bus on one of its mystery tours, anything.

High on his observation point, Graham watched the Killing Pits Club members as they tackled the bend.

Out of the first cars to come through, three had reduced their onwards rush to a safe speed and they had safely negotiated the bend even if they had lost a few precious seconds. They were local lads who knew the corner well but another, Don Castle, had raced around at full speed to clip the nearside verge and veer across to the offside as his front wheels had been thrown out of line. But Don was a good driver — he'd not panicked. He'd corrected the error, changed down two gears and roared away with a toot of his horn for Graham.

Graham looked at his watch.

Another car was due any second now. He had a piece of paper ready to record the registration number and the time it passed the sycamore tree at the far side of the road. That tree was his marker — he timed them as the bonnet reached that point. He heard a car in the distance, a noisy vehicle, and it was heading this way. It didn't sound as lively as the earlier ones.

Graham settled down to his task. It was just after four o'clock, he noted, but the oncoming vehicle was not yet in sight. He rose onto tiptoe to peer across the stubbly heather, wondering which of them had such a noisy old vehicle. It sounded something like Denis' dad's car, a bit rough, in need of some attention to the engine or piston rings . . . and then he saw it. It *was* Denis' dad's car and it was hurtling towards the dip in the road as if it was heading for a straight, level length of a race track. It was going far too fast . . .

Horrified, Graham looked at the other side of the dip. A car was coming in the opposite direction! God! It was heading into the dip too, heading towards Denis. It was like his mum's car . . . the same colour, same model . . . a woman was driving.

Oh my God, he breathed. It was his mother! Graham looked at Denis, but Denis was not looking around himself. His entire concentration was locked upon the dangers ahead. He was keeping the car on the road, hurtling towards Bracken Corner far too fast. Graham ran higher to warn his mother. He reached a hillock and stood there waving his hands and shouting . . . she was not looking away from the road either, doubtless concentrating upon the difficult corner which lay ahead.

And then she saw him. The movement of his arms attracted her attention and, for a second, she took her eyes off the road and stared at him. Her son! Here? What was Graham doing in the middle of the moor, waving his arms like that? Had he been stranded? Lost on a walk?

In those puzzling, awful but extremely brief moments, Joan took her eyes off the road and this small but crucial action caused her car to veer to the wrong side of the carriageway. It was a narrow track, but it was just wide enough for two cars to pass if each took care, if each drove slowly and if each took to the verge with their nearside wheels. But when two cars were heading towards each other with one racing and the other on the wrong side of the road, horror lay in wait.

"Mother, stop! Stop, stop, stop!" shouted Graham, but his words were wasted on the crisp air of the March afternoon and as Mrs Forrester entered the final stage of that severe bend, so did Denis.

It was too late when Denis saw her coming. She was fuzzy, he was dizzy, she was on the wrong side of the road and he was going too fast . . . he braked, she braked, the two cars skidded towards each other in what looked like slow motion and then there was a sickening crash.

Denis felt metal work crushing him, he smelt petrol, he heard screams and the noise of rending metal, of roaring engines and then a deep, calming blackness descended. And as he blacked out, the last thing he saw was Mrs Forrester's head, bloody and shocking, as it crashed through the windscreen of the car which was embedded in his.

* * *

On the hill above it all, Graham had no idea what to do. The sickening thud of the two cars made him feel ill; the sight of his mother's head crashing into the windscreen . . . Denis lying there, white and not moving, and the awful tangle of metal, the smell of petrol, the hiss of a split tyre.

Crying with anguish, Graham Blaketon ran to help his mum. And somewhere above him, a skylark began to sing.

CHAPTER XI

Graham had no idea what to do. If only his father were here, he would know. He would take control and remain calm and do all the important things, like first aid and calling for ambulances and stemming the flow of blood and switching off petrol supplies and, well, just coping . . . but Graham realised he had no idea how to do those things, how to do anything.

He tried to reach his mother, tried to speak to her, to give her comfort, but the mangled wreckage of the two cars, interlocked in their hissing, creaking world of metal, prevented him. Her door was jammed, she was lying at a grotesque angle and he daren't move her anyway; she seemed to be partially hidden among the tangle of metal, seat fittings and luggage.

In the dim recesses of his mind, he'd heard his father saying how dangerous it was to move badly injured people. You could do a lot of harm by moving the seriously injured if you were inexperienced. That was the doctor's job, casualties had to be moved so very carefully to prevent further damage and so he knew, in spite of his concern, that he must not attempt to render any first aid or move his mother. She was alive, that was one consolation, because she was groaning softly to herself.

Her head looked terrible because it had crashed against the windscreen, though. There was a lot of blood too.

She was now lying with her face among shattered pieces of glass with her blood seeping out from somewhere.

Graham ran to Denis . . . he was trapped too. He was groaning as well but there seemed to be no blood around his head or body . . . but that didn't mean anything. Serious internal injuries could occur without any sign of outward bleeding — that was something else he'd learned from listening to his father talking about the many incidents he'd had to deal with over the years. But all that listening hadn't prepared Graham for this; nothing had. This was the sort of thing that happened to other people, not to you and your family.

Leaving the casualties, Graham ran to his vantage point, seeking a telephone kiosk or a house or a farmstead or a passing car or a hiker or a cyclist — anyone who would call the emergency services. There was no one here now, not a solitary person, not a house in sight. One of his mates from the Killing Pits Club would be along soon, he knew that; it would be the person who was due to leave Aidensfield one minute after Denis. Graham dithered . . . so where the hell was that lad and his car? Surely a minute had passed by now.

He didn't know whether or not to leave the scene, to abandon his mother and Denis in their agony but his instinct told him to stay. Sooner or later, a car would come along this road, and that would be quicker than rushing off to find a telephone in this deserted part of the moorland. Who knew what might happen if he left the scene?

He couldn't leave his mother to her fate, could he? Then he heard a car. It was coming from Aidensfield and judging by the sound it was making it was the Killing Pits Club member who would be following Denis. Graham ran into the road and the moment he saw the car hurtling over the horizon, he waved his arms and shouted for it to slow down and stop.

It was Charlie Stephens doing the Killing Pits circuit; his face was a mask of concentration as he forced his big Vauxhall to the limit along these lanes but the moment he saw Graham, he slammed on his brakes. The car slewed across the road in a terrifying skid but Charlie, a garage mechanic by trade, was sufficiently skilled to bring it to a safe halt.

"What the hell are you doing, Graham?" he shouted from the window. "Trying to get killed or something? Jumping into the road like that . . ."

"In the dip, a hell of a collision," gasped Graham, the words having difficulty in forming. "Head-on. The road's blocked. It's my mum in her car and Denis . . . it's awful Charlie, we need the police, ambulance, a doctor . . ."

Charlie reacted with commendable speed; he left his car to take a quick look at the scene, realised from the damage that was immediately visible that it was a very serious situation and said, "Right, you stay here. Slow other cars down otherwise there'll be a worse pile-up. Leave it to me, I'll ring Ashfordly Police."

"No," cried Graham. "There's no point. The office is shut today, and Aidensfield as well. They're all out at Whitby, at the football match. You'll have to ring Whitby, get an ambulance from there as well."

"Right," and Charlie returned to his car, reversed onto a patch of flat moorland, turned his car around within seconds and was tearing back to Aidensfield with lights blazing. He must warn any oncoming vehicles, find a telephone and get help.

Graham went back to his mother.

He felt so useless. All he could do was to say, "Help's on the way, Mum . . . I'm sorry . . ."

But she made no reply as the blood drained from her.

* * *

Charlie's call for help was received at Whitby Police Station in Spring Hill. It was a red-brick Victorian edifice on the narrow, cobbled lane just below the hospital and the office duty constable, a calm voiced man called Finch, listened and said, "All right, Mr Stephens, I'll have someone sent out immediately. Can you return to the scene and give whatever help is needed in the meantime?"

"Sure," consented Charlie. The first thing he'd do was to find a breakdown vehicle because something powerful would be needed to haul those cars apart, then he'd go and stop all oncoming traffic at the scene. Some of those Killing Pits Club members might not be quite as skilled as he, and might plough into the wreckage . . . God, he hoped Graham was coping out there.

PC Finch knew that Inspector Murchison was on duty at the football ground and although she was not in radio contact with Whitby Police Station, she could be reached by telephone. Finch rang the ground and asked the club secretary to find Inspector Murchison and bring her to the telephone.

"She's right here beside me," was the response. "I'll put her on."

When Inspector Murchison responded, Finch said, "We've a report of a traffic accident, ma'am, near Aidensfield, at a place called Bracken Corner. Two injured persons, both serious by the sound of it. I've called the ambulance. We need an officer to attend, they're at the match."

"Right, I'll send Sergeant Blaketon and the Ashfordly car, I'm sure we can manage without him and his men while the crowds are departing."

"Very good, ma'am."

And so the emergency services were alerted. The ambulance service responded immediately, despatching one vehicle and two crew members to the scene without delay. They would make an assessment to see if a doctor was required, but in the meantime, the casualty department of Whitby Cottage Hospital had been warned of the impending arrival of two badly injured patients. While that was happening, Inspector Murchison ran out of the football ground to find Sergeant Blaketon. With as much dignity as she could muster, she ran down the street to hail Blaketon.

He was standing with his back to the high fence, feeling very bored and very useless; Ventress had kept asking why they couldn't go home because there was nothing to do here and suggested they all disappear for a cup of tea while Nick's preoccupation seemed to be the score. At the moment, it was still one-nil to Whitby and then Nick noticed the inspector heading towards them, her large, ungainly figure looking hilarious as she tried to gallop with some dignity.

"The new inspector's in a bit of a flap," grinned Nick. "Do you think she's coming to warn us that the game's nearly over? To warn us to get ready for a rush of departing fans?"

"She'll do herself an injury, running like that," grinned Blaketon.

"Sergeant, Sergeant Blaketon," she was calling to him. "There's a serious traffic accident near Aidensfield, Bracken Corner. Two injuries, a head-on collision. The ambulance has been called. I think you should deal with it, it is in your section."

"No more details, ma'am?"

"No, that's all we have at the moment."

"Right, no sooner said than done. Rowan, Ventress, we've work to do. Into the car immediately!"

"Yes, Sergeant," they chorused and each ran towards the waiting Ford, thankful they had something positive to occupy them instead of just hanging around the streets. This was better than car parking at a football match!

But even as they climbed into the car, with Blaketon at the wheel, the crowd in the ground erupted into loud cheers.

"Another goal!" shouted Nick.

"But who's scored?" grunted Ventress. "Don't say Crook's gone and scored!"

"We've no time to worry about football scores at a time like this," smiled Blaketon. "This is real police work, Ventress. Right, Rowan, which is the quickest way to Bracken Corner?"

* * *

As the emergency services were heading across the moors towards Aidensfield, various forms of assistance had arrived at Bracken Corner. One was, by chance, a passing doctor who was on holiday in the area. He instructed the others that under no circumstances should Mrs Forrester be moved from her car until the ambulance arrived. He'd remain to supervise the ambulance staff, although he did express an opinion, after crawling around the interlocked vehicles, that the cars could be hauled apart without harming the patients, if it was done gently. Access to the injured parties would then be easier. A local farmer, en route to the village, stopped on his tractor and soon he was coiling a powerful chain around the bumper of Denis' car, while a delivery van driver halted and came to help the farmer. Other people arrived too, including several members of the Killing Pits Club who had been attempting the fastest tour of the circuit.

There were assorted onlookers too, motorists, a party of hikers and some local people who had come along to see what was happening. Scenes like this always attracted crowds; ghouls, the police called them.

First of the official emergency services to arrive was the ambulance. Parking their vehicle as close as possible, the two ambulancemen, reacting calmly and very efficiently to the situation, were guided to the casualties. The doctor, whose name was Rowe, said that Mrs Forrester could be moved, albeit on a stretcher, and that the young man was not so badly hurt. The ambulancemen, with their stretcher at the door of Mrs Forrester's car, began to tenderly extricate her from the wreckage while the doctor supported her wherever he could. In a surprisingly short time, she was lying on the stretcher with the doctor continuing to monitor her as she was being carried to the waiting ambulance.

"She is a very sick woman," he warned them. "She must go to hospital without delay — you'll radio ahead for casualty to be prepared for her arrival? She'll require immediate emergency treatment and her loss of blood is very serious."

"We've time to recover the lad as well?" queried one of the ambulancemen.

"Sure, yes, of course but be quick, every second counts."

And so Denis Myers, still unconscious, was removed from his badly damaged car and at this point, some of his injuries became evident.

His left arm hung at an awkward angle and his face was bleeding and bruised where he'd been lying on some broken glass. With the same tenderness they'd shown to Mrs Forrester, Denis was laid upon a stretcher and rushed across to the waiting ambulance. Its engine was already running and the rear doors were open. Under the expert guidance of the willing doctor, the two casualties were eased into their positions, one at either side of the ambulance, as the two ambulancemen began to secure the stretchers to their base.

During these events, Graham Blaketon had been wandering around like a lost sheep. Sometimes he'd gone across to his Killing Pits friends, amongst whom Gordon had appeared, and sometimes he peered into the distance as if awaiting his father, but all the time he was unable to say anything. He seemed to be in a daze and then someone said, "Here's the police, about bloody time too!"

"Don't move the cars any more," Doctor Rowe said. "The police will want to see them in position."

Graham saw the small black car coming closer and when it was a few yards from the damaged cars, Sergeant Blaketon eased it onto the verge. Putting on his cap, he emerged from the car as Graham ran across to break the awful news.

"It's mum," were his first words.

"Your mum, Joan? Where?" asked Blaketon.

"In the accident, she's in the ambulance . . . Denis ran into her, Dad . . . it was awful," and Graham broke down.

Tears began to roll down his face as he sobbed beyond control, and so, tenderly, Sergeant Blaketon said, "Go and sit in my car, son, I'll see you in a moment or two, it seems I've got work to do."

Nick came to his sergeant's side.

"Serge," he said quietly. "Did I hear right? Is it Mrs Blaketon who's been hurt?"

"Yes, Rowan, it is my former wife, her name's Forrester now. Now, you and Ventress go and assume control of the situation while I have words with the ambulancemen. I need to establish the seriousness of the situation."

Nick could see that his sergeant was having a struggle to contain his emotions; to be confronted with the fact that your wife, or ex-wife, was a casualty in a serious traffic accident must be terrible. Blaketon was clearly displaying an enormous degree of self-control as he strode across to the ambulance. Just as he reached it, one of the men was closing the door. Nick decided he would stay a moment or two at his sergeant's side. As the ambulanceman was walking away, Sergeant Blaketon reached for the handle and began to open the door. "Sergeant!" snapped the driver. "No, not now! There'll be time for interviews later, this is an emergency."

"It's my wife," he said softly. "Well, ex-wife to be precise."

"Oh, I'm sorry," the ambulanceman now appreciated the awful agony of the policeman's situation.

"Can I see her?" asked Blaketon.

"For ten seconds, Sergeant, no more. I must get her to hospital, she's lost an awful lot of blood," and he began to unlock the door. Sergeant Blaketon climbed inside and looked upon Joan. He was devastated by what he saw and broke down in tears. The ambulance driver was hovering near the door, uncertain how to react but anxious to get his patient into casualty without further delay.

Nick spoke to the ambulanceman, "He can go to the hospital with you, can't he? Sergeant Blaketon? Being a relative?"

"Yes, sure, we'll take him."

"And the son?"

"Yes, tell him to get in now, front seat will be fine. Then we must go, really we must."

"Sergeant," Nick shouted into the rear of the vehicle. "Stay there, go to the hospital with her. Graham's coming as well."

Blaketon tried to put on a brave face in his dilemma, and said, "You can cope, can you?"

"I'm in control, Sergeant, I'm an Ashfordly section officer, remember? The cream of Ashfordly section, that's me and Alf. Of course we can cope."

"Right, I'll go with her. I must, it's such a shock . . ."

"Graham," Nick shouted across to the lad in the police car. "Get into the front seat, you're off to hospital with your mum and dad. Look after them, son, they both need you!" Without a word, Graham obeyed and once the Blaketons were all aboard, the driver switched on his blue rotating light and the ambulance eased away smoothly for its swift run to Whitby's Cottage Hospital.

"So, what happened here, Alf?" Nick asked as the two constables began their task of dealing with the aftermath.

They took measurements, asking bystanders for statements of evidence but none had witnessed the accident. He saw members of the Killing Pits Club who were standing some distance away and went across to them. He asked after Gordon, but someone said he'd come and gone, taking his motorbike with him, saying Graham didn't need it any more.

One by one, Nick asked if any of them had witnessed the accident, but none had. Then he asked whether Denis had been racing, whether Denis had a full driving licence and what he was doing with his father's car, but no one could enlighten Nick.

"Well," said Nick after his abortive quizzing of them. "You have not been very helpful, and we do have a very seriously injured woman as a result of this. I fully intend to find out exactly what did happen here today, and exactly what Denis was doing. I will visit you each individually starting this evening. I will find out what happened, mark my words."

From the available evidence at the scene, however, such as dirt on the road, debris and broken glass, Nick was able to identify the precise point of impact.

That was most important for his report and having achieved that, he gave permission for the breakdown truck to remove the battered cars from their present resting places. Now the road could be opened to traffic again, but as Mrs

Forrester's car was being hauled upon the platform of the breakdown vehicle, Nick could see the skid marks it had left on the surface of the road, seconds before impact.

"Alf," he said with some sorrow. "See that?"

"What?" asked Alf.

"She was on the wrong side of the road," said Nick.

CHAPTER XII

While Nick Rowan and Alf Ventress were examining the scene of the accident and gathering evidence for the report that Nick would eventually submit, Sergeant Blaketon held the unconscious Joan's hand as the ambulance swiftly but smoothly conveyed her and Denis to hospital. One ambulanceman was in attendance as the other drove; he monitored Joan's stertorous breathing as Blaketon sat in shocked silence.

There was so little Blaketon could do. For the first time in his professional life, he felt useless. That knowledge was made worse by the fact that the victim was the woman he had loved and still loved. He gripped her hand gently, but there was no corresponding response from her.

Graham was in the front passenger seat, saying nothing to anyone because his entire concern was whether or not his mother would survive. Never before had he seen such injuries; he'd seen plenty of scrubs, cuts and bruises at school, and one of his footballing pals once broke a leg, but it had been nothing compared with this. Graham had also seen his father's reaction to those injuries — that alone revealed that his mother was in an extremely serious condition. The thought of what had happened to her, and his part in the drama, caused a tear to well up within his eye. He began to weep in silence, wiping his eyes and hoping the driver wouldn't notice.

He tried to settle down for the awful journey to hospital, he tried to think what his father might have done if he'd been first at the scene, but the longer the journey, the more Graham brooded over his unhappy role in this terrible drama. If only he hadn't left Denis with the others, if only Denis hadn't taken those pills, if only Denis hadn't driven so fast into that corner, if only his mother hadn't swerved . . .

At the hospital, the ambulance turned smoothly into the casualty department's entrance and reversed into the necessary bay as the team of waiting experts moved quickly into action. They had been forewarned of this admission, they knew Joan needed immediate and highly skilled surgery, coupled with an urgent blood transfusion. Joan, immobile upon her stretcher, was swiftly carried into the hospital and taken straight to the theatre.

"If you gentlemen would like to wait in reception," said one of the ambulancemen to the Blaketons. "Someone will come and see you. Please be patient, it might take some time."

Sergeant Blaketon knew his way around the hospital and led his silent unhappy son into the depths of the building through a series of stark corridors until they arrived at the reception desk. A nurse smiled at them.

"Yes, Sergeant?" she asked. "Can I help you?"

"The traffic accident," he said somewhat nervously. "We're here with Mrs Forrester, she's just been taken into theatre. It was at Aidensfield . . ."

"I'm afraid you will not be able to interview her, Sergeant . . ." she pulled a form from a drawer and began to complete the heading. "Now, if you are dealing with the accident, you'll be able to help me. What is the lady's full name and address, and who are the next of kin?"

"We are," he said. "The casualty is my ex-wife, and this is our son. I'm not here to interview her, I'm here to give her support. My name is Blaketon, Oscar Blaketon from

Ashfordly Police Station and this is our son, Graham; she is now called Mrs Forrester, she married again, you see."

"Oh, I'm sorry, Sergeant, I thought . . ."

"Yes, I know," he said. "People of my profession usually come here to interview witnesses. There was another young man too, in the accident."

"His name is Denis Myers," said Graham, trying to be useful. "He lives at Aidensfield," and Graham gave details of the Myers' home address.

"Thank you, I'll let the doctor know you are both here, Sergeant, and we'll try to get word to Mr Myers' parents." When the nurse had completed the necessary paperwork from the details they supplied, she indicated some chairs and said, "If you'd like to wait here, I'll get the doctor to visit you. Now, a cup of tea?"

"Thank you, yes. Milk, no sugar, for us both."

Sergeant Blaketon, cap in hand, moved across to the row of chairs, nodded to a young couple who were already waiting there, and sat down, placing his cap on the chair at his side. Graham joined him.

"Dad, I . . . I mean . . . it was awful . . . I was there, I saw it."

"Accidents happen, son," said Blaketon. "I just hope she pulls through."

"But Dad, I feel as if I'm to blame . . ."

"You mustn't, Graham. It would be that other lad's fault, Denis, driving like hell, I bet. You know what lads are like. But Rowan's in control, he'll find out what happened, so don't you fret about it. She needs us here, both of us. We're all she's got now."

And so Graham lapsed into a deep silence, tortured by his own thoughts. He was plagued by images of his mother driving along the wrong side of the road and of Denis racing into that corner . . . and then he had vision after vision of that terrible collision. He sat with his head in his hands as a nurse arrived with two cups of tea and some biscuits on a tray. Blaketon took the tray and set it on an empty chair, then touched Graham's shoulder before silently handing him a cup.

Then Kate Rowan, in her white coat and bearing a clipboard, entered the reception area. She smiled at Sergeant Blaketon and Graham, but it was not a smile of happiness or of confidence. The grim expression on her face revealed the thoughts in her own mind, thoughts based on professional skill.

Blaketon placed his cup on a chair and rose to meet her. Graham copied his father.

"Sergeant Blaketon, I'm so sorry . . . I had no idea it was Joan, not at first, not until the ambulanceman explained," Kate spoke gently to him.

"How is she?" were his first words.

"She's a very sick woman, Sergeant. Extremely sick, it would be wrong of me to pretend otherwise. Obviously, we don't yet know the full extent of her injuries, the surgeon is examining her now, but from a preliminary examination there appears to be a very serious head injury, along with some internal damage and a worrying loss of blood. She is in very good hands, I can assure you, and you know we will do our very best for her."

"You'll be looking after her?" asked Blaketon with some hope in his voice. "You, in person, I mean?"

"No, not in person. I'm just one of the team, Sergeant, I'm not the resident doctor here. You know I've joined a practice in Whitby, with Jim Radcliffe — Doctor James Radcliffe that is. I work in Whitby from time to time, and hospital work forms part of our duties. But I'm not a surgeon."

"Can I see her?" Blaketon's voice almost broke with emotion. "Well, that is, can we see her?"

"Not at the moment, Sergeant, not while she's in theatre, but the moment she comes out, I'll see what I can do. It could be a long wait, I'm afraid."

"Yes, of course, I understand."

"Does Nick know?" she asked. "He was in Whitby this afternoon, on football duties."

"We were called out to deal with the accident, me, your husband and PC Ventress that is. PC Rowan is there now, at the scene, dealing with the accident and its aftermath."

"Oh, Sergeant, I'm so sorry. That must be awful, finding your loved one's been hurt like this."

"Yes, it was a shock, a deep, deep shock," and tears welled in the tough sergeant's eyes, as Kate took his arm and settled him back onto a chair.

"We'll do all we can," she said quietly, as she walked back to her ministrations. But there were tears in her own eyes as she turned away from Oscar Blaketon. As she walked away, he realised he'd forgotten to ask about the condition of Denis Myers.

* * *

At the scene, most of the bystanders had dispersed. The two wrecked cars, having been inspected by the police at the scene, were now en route via separate breakdown vehicles to a garage for a more detailed examination by experts. Matters like the condition of the brakes, steering and tyres would be scrutinised and a report would be compiled for eventual use in court, should any prosecution or prosecutions result from the accident.

Nick and Alf remained at the scene because, when everything had been cleared away, someone had to sweep the roads clear of broken glass, bits of metal and mud. And unless the police did it, no one else would.

And so, as evidence of the drama disappeared piece by piece from the scene, Alf and Nick got to work. There was a broom and shovel in the boot of the police car, just some of the equipment that every police car carried. But as the two constables busied themselves in those final moments, Nick realised that two youngsters were still standing on the moor, watching them.

He knew them only by their first names, Duncan and Janet; they were a decent couple who were everywhere together and Nick knew they were members of the Killing Pits Club. As he and Alf cleared away the debris and placed it in a hessian sack, another piece of equipment from their car, Duncan came over to Nick.

"Mr Rowan," he said quietly. "This is awful . . . I'm not sure what to say."

"It's Denis who has the questions to answer," Nick said quietly. "He's the one who was driving."

"I'm going to do something about that club," said Duncan seriously. "We'll have to put a stop to all this."

"Time trialling, you mean?" said Nick.

"You know about it?"

"Knowing about it and proving it are not quite the same thing, Duncan, but I think this will have taught some of your members a harsh lesson — at a huge cost as well, judging by the state of Sergeant Blaketon's Joan. But I appreciate your concern. And I think it would be a good idea to have that club run on proper lines; it would be something positive for the youngsters and would give them guidance."

"I'll think about that, but what I really wanted to say was sorry; sorry to the Blaketons and Myers," said Duncan. "All the club carries responsibility for what happened."

"I'll speak to Sergeant Blaketon when this is all over," Nick assured him. "I know he'll appreciate what you've just said."

As Duncan returned to Janet on the moorland overlooking the scene, Nick joined Alf in the police car and they drove away towards Ashfordly.

"I'll drop you off at your house," offered Alf. "I can deal with things at the Ashfordly end, I'll ring Whitby with a situation report, just to complete their occurrence book entry."

"And I'll submit the accident report in due course," said Nick as the car gathered speed. "But it was good of young Duncan to speak like that — it makes you realise there are some decent youngsters in the world."

"Try telling that to Joan Forrester," grunted Alf.

As the police car drove away from the scene, Duncan turned to Janet and hugged her.

"PC Rowan's right, Janet. What we need is a proper motoring club," he said. "One that teaches the kids how to drive properly; if they want excitement, we might get ourselves into motor rallies, proper ones, I mean, or maybe a day on an old airfield if they want to race."

"Then let's get something organised, Duncan," said his fresh-faced girl. "We can do it, you and me! We don't need Gordon and all his posturing!"

"Where is Gordon?" asked Duncan. "I thought he was here?"

"He was," she said. "He got a lift when he heard about the accident, but then left almost as soon as he arrived, he took his bike away."

"Guilty feelings, eh? Can't cope with real trouble, can he?" snapped Duncan.

And as they turned to leave the scene, there being no one else on the moor at that time, Janet noticed something lying in the heather fairly close to the road.

"Look, there's a parcel!" she pointed to it. "All wrapped up nicely in brown paper, and it's got a tag on!"

She ran down the slope to retrieve the object.

"It's heavy, it feels like a book," she said, fingering the edges. "And there's a note . . . 'To Oscar, wishing you a happy birthday, love Joan and Graham'. It's not wet or dirty, so it hasn't been here long."

"It must have been thrown out of one of those cars," said Duncan. "We'll hand it in. We can give it to PC Rowan, he'll know what to do with it."

"Right," she agreed, taking his arm.

* * *

When Nick returned to his police house in Aidensfield, it was deserted and in darkness. He knew Kate was undertaking duties at Whitby, performing tasks which now formed part of her enlarged partnership practice, and he wondered if she was aware of the identity of the casualties of the accident. She might even be dealing with them. As Nick wondered what to do about something to eat, the telephone rang. "Aidensfield Police," he answered. "PC Rowan."

"It's Gerry Brownlow," said the voice. "Sorry to disturb you, Nick, but somebody's broken into our offertory box."

"Oh, no!" groaned Nick. "Much gone?"

"I wouldn't think so. By this stage of the week, there's usually £3 or £4 in, not much more. They've smashed open the box lid with a jemmy or a big screwdriver or something."

"When was it last checked?" asked Nick.

"I came in just after lunch," said Brownlow. "It was OK then."

"OK, Gerry, I'll come down to examine it. You'll be at the church?"

"Sure."

"In half an hour then."

Nick next rang Whitby Hospital to check on the condition of Joan Forrester and Denis Myers. He was told that Mrs Forrester's condition was giving cause for alarm, but that Denis Myers was not too badly hurt. He was conscious now and out of danger, although he was suffering from a broken left arm and abrasions. He was in the men's general ward. Nick also learned that Sergeant Blaketon and Graham were still at the hospital, waiting.

In addition to Joan Forrester and Denis Myers, Nick had to interview Graham Blaketon. Graham was the only witness to the accident, other than the two injured parties, so he must be interviewed. He wasn't injured and could therefore be interviewed at the hospital tonight, so Nick decided that if he had to go out to visit Thackerston church, then he might as well continue to Whitby. He could then see if he could conclude any of the necessary interviews.

He rang Ashfordly Police Station.

"Alf," he said. "I've just had a call from the churchwarden of Thackerston church. It's been raided, a few quid gone. Usual method of entry to the offertory box. I'm on my way there after I've snatched a sandwich, and then I'm going to the hospital at Whitby to see if I can get some interviews completed, young Blaketon in particular."

"Right you are, Nick, all's quiet at this end."

And so, after a ham sandwich and a quick cup of tea, Nick set about his Saturday night's duties.

His enquiries at Thackerston church did not reveal much information. Gerry Brownlow could not help, other than to say he'd seen the box earlier that afternoon when it was secure. He hadn't heard any sounds of a motorbike in the village during the afternoon, but as he'd been cutting his lawn his own noise might have drowned that of any visitor. He did say, however, that a scruffy individual with a long khaki greatcoat, accompanied by a greyish coloured flea-ridden dog of some kind, had volunteered to mow the long grass among the graves. Brownlow had agreed, but felt sure the fellow had not robbed the offertory box — that man had come this morning, and had left the premises by lunch time.

Nick acquainted Mr Brownlow with the current situation concerning such thefts and advised him to persuade the church authorities to encase the replacement box within the wall. If it was made of tough metal, and cemented into the framework of the church, it should deter future thieves.

Nick then mounted his Francis Barnett and headed for Whitby. He was not looking forward to his interview with Graham Blaketon, partly because Sergeant Blaketon would be in attendance but especially because Graham's mother was the casualty and his friend was the other driver involved. Just how independent would Graham be? How reliable would be any statement he made?

And why had his mother crossed to the wrong side of the road? That alone suggested a careless driving charge against her. And what of Denis Myers?

Nick would have to check his driving licence because he was sure Denis had never passed a test, nor did he own a car. Somewhat wearily, Nick realised he had a lot of enquiries to make about Denis and about other matters associated with that accident.

As he left Aidensfield behind, he wondered how Kate was coping at Whitby.

CHAPTER XIII

After undergoing emergency surgery, in particular the efforts to stem heavy internal bleeding, Joan Forrester was returned to a quiet ward. Heavily bandaged around the head, and with her body dressings less evident, she lay between the crisp white sheets with one arm on top; a drip was affixed to that arm and she was absorbing a transfusion of new and desperately needed blood. It would be one of many. Almost as pale as the sheets themselves, she lay immobile as Kate looked upon her.

There was no indication that Joan Forrester would recover consciousness in the near future and so Kate decided that Sergeant Blaketon and Graham could see her now. At least she looked at rest, peaceful and clean. Kate went through to the reception area and located father and son.

"You can see her now," she said gently.

"How is she?" asked Blaketon.

"Sleeping," said Kate. "The surgery was a success — well, I mean, as successful as we could make it under the circumstances, but she is far from well. I do not wish to build up any false hopes, Sergeant. I must tell you that she is dangerously ill. But you may see her now. She will not respond to you, I'm afraid."

Kate led them along the corridors to the ward where Joan lay alone in a bed; Blaketon's practised eyes immediately noticed the drip, the charts, the oxygen mask, the bell push beside the bed and the range of sophisticated equipment.

Joan was lying asleep, her face showing a remarkable calmness and a lack of concern or pain. Father and son moved to the bedside, Blaketon with his arm around his son's shoulders, and they said nothing. Kate waited in the background, not wishing to intrude upon their moments of privacy and yet not wishing to leave in case she was required. But after two minutes, Blaketon turned to her and said, "Thank you, doctor. May we wait a little longer? In case she does recover consciousness?"

"It might be several hours, Sergeant, and even then she might not recognise you. She has undergone a terrible experience and, well, I'm afraid I cannot build up your hopes, either of you . . ."

"You are saying she might die?" Blaketon asked.

"Yes, Sergeant. That's exactly what I am saying."

"Thank you for being so honest. Come along, Graham, we'll wait outside. Thanks for letting us see her, Kate."

He called her Kate in a rare moment of friendship, something he had never done before, and Kate's lips quivered with emotion. Poor Oscar . . . he was finding this most difficult; it would do him good to have a long weep himself, but she knew he would never do that.

Not in uniform, anyway, and not in front of his son. While admiring him for his strong self-control, she did think that a show of emotion would ease his agony and be beneficial in the long term.

When the Blaketons had left, Kate went through to the men's ward to visit Denis Myers. As she walked in, a nurse was tucking the sheets around him and he was sitting up in bed. One arm was in a sling, and there was a bandage over his left eye and around his head. His face and hands showed evidence of cuts and abrasions but he was fully conscious and surprisingly alert.

"Hello, Denis," Kate smiled as she approached. "Just let me take your temperature, then we can talk."

She asked him to take the thermometer in his mouth, checked the reading and said, "Fine. You seem to be very strong, Denis, but you were a very lucky young man. You got off lightly, you know."

"She was on the wrong side of the road, doctor. I never stood a chance. It wasn't my fault, so it's good news I'm not too badly hurt."

"You shouldn't have been driving, Denis," Kate reminded him. "I warned you, remember? When I prescribed those antihistamine tablets, I told you not to drink alcohol and not to drive."

"They didn't do any harm!" he was most belligerent. "They didn't affect my driving!"

"Of course they affected your driving! They affected your judgement too! You should *not* have been driving that car, Denis, and you know it. I gave you a distinct and very clear warning."

"No you didn't!"

"Denis, how can you say that? We always warn people who take antihistamines, it's so important that we tell them of the dangers. And I told you, I know I did."

"I'll say you never," he snapped. "If I get taken to court over this, I'll say you never warned me about the tablets."

"Denis, how could you! You know it's not true!"

"Nobody's blaming me for running into that woman! It was her fault, all her fault."

"The police will decide who was responsible, Denis, from all the evidence. And Mrs Blaketon . . . er, Mrs Forrester as she now is, is extremely ill. She might die, Denis. It is really that serious."

He looked at her with cold eyes.

"Blaketon you say?"

"Graham's mother, it was Graham's mother in that other car, Denis, Sergeant Blaketon's former wife. She is very ill indeed."

"So she was a copper's ex-wife. They'll gang up against me, won't they? They'll make it seem I was in the wrong. What chance do I have, eh? Against them. But I'll not have it. She was on the wrong side of the bloody road, Doctor Rowan."

"I'm sure the police will elicit the truth," she said.

He began to shout, "You'd better make sure your husband knows that! That she was on the wrong side of the road. And you never warned me about driving after the tablets, right? You never, that's what I'll say. You never, you never!"

Kate could not believe what she was hearing.

"You'd better try and rest, Denis," she said, deciding not to argue any further. After all, Denis was undergoing treatment so perhaps he was not too rational. And he was still suffering from the shock of the event. She left him without another word, but she was very upset at what he'd alleged. If he repeated his allegations in court, it would look as if she was failing her duty as a doctor. It was so easy to make such an allegation but so much more difficult to disprove it.

Kate returned to the office she was using in the hospital and settled behind the desk. God, this was awful! She *had* told Denis not to drive, she had told him that the pills would cause dizziness but in spite of her warnings, he had driven that car! And he was only a learner driver.

As she sat with her head in her hands, there was a knock on the door. Taking a deep breath, she sat erect in her chair and called "Come in."

It was Nick, in full uniform and the moment he saw his wife, he realised she was unhappy.

"Kate?" he frowned as he strode across to her.

She hurried to him and clung to him as he took her in his arms and suddenly she was weeping.

"Kate?" he kissed her tenderly on the forehead. "Kate, what is it?"

"Oh, it's nothing, I shouldn't let people like Denis get to me!"

"Denis? You mean Denis Myers? Why, what's he done?"

"He claimed I never warned him about driving after some tablets I'd prescribed. They make you dizzy, Nick, they're antihistamines, so when you're on a course of them, you're not supposed to drive. I warned Denis, and he says I didn't. Now look what's happened!"

"I came here to interview him, Kate."

"Oh, no, I can't allow that, sorry. He's not fit to be interviewed, Nick. As his doctor, I must refuse, at least until he's improved considerably."

"You're protecting him after what he's just done to you?"

"I must never let my professional responsibilities be influenced by my personal feelings, Nick, and you know it. So no interviews of Denis, not yet."

"And how's Joan?"

She took a deep breath and the expression on her face told Nick all he needed to know.

"She's a very sick woman, Nick, and poor old Oscar's taking it very badly. He still loves her, you know, even though they're divorced."

"I know he's taken it hard, he broke down in the ambulance."

"Now he's trying to conceal his sorrow, I wish he'd cry all the more and let his grief come out, but he won't."

"He's a tough old trooper, that's what happens when you are a senior policeman! You overcome grief, you don't let it intrude upon your life, even though it involves your own loved ones. I'll talk to him in due course, but I do need to interview young Graham, Kate, as soon as possible. He was the only witness."

"I can't object to that, Nick, he's with his father, in reception. You can go through if you wish."

"When I've talked to Graham, I'm going home," Nick told her. "How about you? Can you come home soon?"

"I'll have to stay with Joan," Kate said quietly. "I don't know when I can finish for the night."

"She's as serious as that, is she?" Nick put to her.

"Yes," said Kate without elaborating.

Nick took her in his arms, kissed her tenderly and said, "I love you, Kate, I really do."

"And I love you, Nick, I really do. But isn't life cruel? Poor old Oscar and Graham, Graham looks lost . . ."

"He's got his dad, and his dad's got him," Nick said. "They've got each other and that's what's important right now. Well, I must leave you. See you later?"

And he left Doctor Rowan to continue her work while he padded along the corridor to reception. As he entered, he could see Sergeant Blaketon sitting hunched in his chair, cap at his side on another chair, as he stared at the floor. Graham was nearby, also staring at the floor and neither was speaking. Nick entered and glanced at the clock. It was ten minutes to ten, some six hours after the accident, and they were still awaiting any good news of Joan.

Nick moved among the chairs and as he approached his sergeant, he took a chair, twisted it around so that it was facing the opposite direction and sat upon it. He was now facing Blaketon and Graham.

Sergeant Blaketon observed Nick's approach.

"Rowan," he produced a quick slight smile of recognition, of pleasure even, at having someone to talk to.

"I'm sorry, Sergeant, about Joan, er Mrs Forrester."

"She's in good hands, Rowan, and that gives me great comfort. Everyone is so kind, and your wife has been especially good to me, very professional. And you are in control of things? Getting enough evidence for the accident report?"

"Yes, and that's why I am here. I need to talk to Graham," Nick glanced at the youth. "I know it's not a good time, but . . ."

"I'd have done the same myself, Rowan, if things had been different. You have a job to do, so get on and do it!"

Nick turned towards Graham who was steadfastly avoiding Nick's eyes, staring persistently at the floor.

"Graham," Nick spoke quietly and with some sympathy. "I'm sorry about what happened, but I need to know just what did occur. I need you to tell me. You were a witness, I believe, you arranged for someone to call the emergency services, Graham, you did a good job out there."

"I don't know what happened, Mr Rowan," the lad shook his head but never took his eyes off the floor. "I never saw, I don't know."

"I think you do know, Graham. You know what I think? I think Denis was racing, I think he was taking part in one of those Killing Pits time trials, and I think he lost control on that corner . . ."

Graham shook his head and, without raising his eyes to meet those of Nick, whispered, "I just don't know, Mr Rowan, I just don't know! I never saw!"

"Your mum's driving, Graham," Nick persisted. "Was that all right? I mean, was she on the correct side of the road?"

"I never saw, Mr Rowan, I never saw, honest, I never saw a thing . . ."

"So why were you out there on that road? Time-keeping perhaps? For the Killing Pits Club? Letting Denis drive his dad's car even though he hasn't passed his driving test?"

Nick's voice had been rising as he threw the questions at the unhappy youth and he could see that Graham was now on the point of tears. Nick pushed home his advantage.

"Graham, I need to know what happened, and I'm sure you saw everything . . ."

"I saw nothing, I tell you, nothing!" and now Graham burst into tears as his father came across and placed an arm around his shoulder.

"I think that's enough for now, Rowan," said Sergeant Blaketon.

"I'll have to interview him again, Sergeant, I do need a written statement from Graham. He's our only witness."

"Yes, I understand that, but not now eh, Rowan, not now," whispered Sergeant Blaketon, himself showing signs of stress.

And so Nick retreated. He went back to Kate's office to bid farewell to her, but she was not there. He went outside, jumped onto his motorcycle and rode home to an empty house.

* * *

It was some time later, when Graham had recovered a little of his composure, that his father said, "You know, Graham, the only way to make things right is to tell the truth. I'm not going to press you for answers, not now, but if PC Rowan does come seeking the truth of this afternoon's events, you should tell him, however much it hurts, however much you loved your mum or count yourself as a true friend of Denis."

"I couldn't, Dad," he sniffed. "I couldn't, really."

Father and son remained together in that deserted waiting room, the nurse giving them cups of coffee and biscuits as the night hours ticked away. From time to time, Kate Rowan paid them a visit, each time bringing no further news about Joan other than to say she remained unconscious and was not responding to further treatment.

And then, at five o'clock in the morning, a nurse was passing Joan's bed when she noticed that the patient's eyes were open. She went in to speak to Joan.

"Hello, Mrs Forrester."

"Is Oscar there? And Graham?"

"I'm sure they are, I'll go and see."

The nurse went out of the ward to find Kate first; Kate hurried to Joan's bedside and smiled.

"Well, well, Mrs Forrester! Nice to see you smiling. How are you?"

"Tired, doctor, very tired. Are Oscar and Graham there?"

"I've sent someone to fetch them in, I can give them a few minutes with you. You'd like that?"

Joan nodded briefly, her voice very weak, and she did manage a very small smile. Moments passed before Sergeant Blaketon, his cap in his hand, entered somewhat nervously closely followed by Graham. They moved towards her bed, one at each side and then Blaketon bowed down and very gently kissed her on the mouth.

"Hello, Joan," he whispered.

"Hello, Oscar, it was good of you to come."

"How could I not have come?" he spoke hoarsely. "We're both here, Graham's with me," and Blaketon turned his eyes in the direction of his son.

Graham was not sure how to respond, but touched his mother's hand and said, "Hi, Mum, glad you could make it."

"How are you feeling, love?" asked Blaketon.

"As well as can be expected, isn't that what they say in these cases?" smiled Joan. "I feel a bit dizzy and fuzzy, almost as if I'm floating and they've put bandages all over the place. I've no idea what they've done to me, but I don't feel any pain, I don't feel anything, in fact. It's like floating, as if my body isn't mine any more. They've been very kind, you know, very kind indeed."

"I know," smiled Oscar.

"I just wanted to say something to you, Oscar, in front of Graham. I wanted to say that I wasn't a very good wife to you, I should have shown more love, more tolerance. I know I should have supported you in your career, Oscar, you're a very good man. Solid and dependable, but good. I'm proud to have been your wife."

"Joan, don't," Blaketon's suppressed emotions were now close to the surface, but she was continuing.

"And look after Graham, won't you? You're all he's got, he's still only a child, Oscar; your child, our child."

And then, with a smile on her lips, she closed her eyes.

For a moment, there was no reaction from anyone as father and son awaited her next words, but there were no more words. Suddenly, Kate realised what had happened and hurried to the bedside. She tested Joan's pulse, lifted her eyelids to examine her eyes, listened for her breath, but there was nothing.

"I'm sorry, Sergeant, Graham," Kate was close to tears herself. "She's gone. I'm so dreadfully sorry."

And she eased the sheets over Joan's bandaged face. Blaketon, now with tears streaming down his face, lifted Joan's bare hand and pressed it to his lips, keeping it there as the emotions of past and present overwhelmed him.

CHAPTER XIV

On that Sunday morning, breakfast time at the police house in Aidensfield was a miserable affair. Kate hadn't returned from the hospital until seven o'clock and had managed only a couple of hours' sleep. She looked extremely tired and drawn following her terrible night's duty. Nick, although he'd gone to bed around midnight, hadn't slept and the phone call from Kate in the early hours, with the awful news about Mrs Forrester, had meant he'd not slept either. Both of them were subdued and going about their morning routine almost automatically.

Nick was at the cooker, frying eggs, sausages and bacon in his new frying pan while Kate was trying to gather her accoutrements for another visit to Whitby. She needed all her recent notes because, after Mrs Blaketon's death, there would be a lot of paperwork to complete, including a statement for the coroner. There would be an inquest — it was inevitable following a fatal road traffic accident, and there would also have to be a post mortem examination even though Kate and the surgeon could specify the cause of Mrs Forrester's death.

For Nick, the fact that the accident had proved fatal meant additional work for him. He would have to liaise with the coroner, arrange a post mortem on Mrs Forrester, collate the medical evidence and evidence from the scene.

Having done all this, he would have to submit a file to Divisional Headquarters for the superintendent to decide whether or not to prosecute Denis Myers. That would be difficult without a witness statement from Graham because the evidence at the scene suggested Mrs Forrester had been at fault.

"How about some breakfast, Kate?" he asked as he finalised the cooking of his own meal.

"Oh, Nick, I couldn't," she shook her head. "But thanks all the same."

There was a long pause and then he said, "Kate, it wasn't Denis' fault; at least the evidence suggests it wasn't. Joan was driving on the wrong side of the road at the time of the impact. The brake marks prove that. If it was anyone's fault, it was hers."

"She might have swerved at the last minute, Nick. You know and I know that Denis was taking antihistamines which means he'd be incapable of driving correctly. He'd be under the influence of drugs, Nick, and he might have been doing something stupid with the car. Joan might have been trying to avoid him, you can't say it was all her fault, not on what you already know."

"I need an independent witness, Kate, I need somebody who saw it all happen, somebody who was at the scene just before the collision, and the only person who was there is young Blaketon. The trouble is he's saying nothing."

"Give him time, Nick, he's only a youngster and he's probably in a state of shock."

"I appreciate that, but I'm not sure whether we can regard him as an independent witness because his mother was a victim. And, of course, a friend was the other driver. He's hardly independent, is he? But the courts might accept his version of events, if I can get him to talk."

"Perhaps he is being truthful, Nick, perhaps he didn't see exactly what happened."

"I think he did. I think he's protecting his mother, or Denis, or both, or he's taking sides with that Killing Pits

Club. I suppose I could obtain a *subpoena* and compel him to come to court to give evidence, if we ever get that far."

Kate produced one of her quiet smiles. "Nick," she asked. "If you do speak to Graham, ask him if he knew anything about Denis' tablets, will you? Graham is staying with Denis at the Myers' home, so he might have seen Denis taking the pills I prescribed, and Denis might have said something about my warning or my diagnosis. I did give him the necessary warning, Nick, so how can I prove it? It's my word against his."

"I'm going down to Ashfordly next, I expect Graham's staying with his father, so I'll try again to get him to talk. So what are your plans today?"

"I've some things to finish off in Whitby, at the hospital and also a surgery to take for Doctor Radcliffe. Barring the unknown, I should be home by lunchtime."

"Me too. Maybe we can have an evening off? Go out somewhere? For a bar snack and a drink? We need to get away from the telephone and from work, if only for the evening."

"I'll see how I feel when I get back. At the moment, all I need is lots of sleep!"

"You'll be treating Denis Myers at the hospital today?" he asked.

"Yes, he'll have to remain there for another day or two."

"Then you will tell me when he's fit to be interviewed, won't you?" he smiled.

"You know I will!"

"So how was Sergeant Blaketon last night when you left him?"

"Very shocked, Nick. He's taking it very badly. He stayed at the hospital for an hour or more after Joan passed away, and Graham stayed with him, then they both went home. Blaketon said he was taking Graham with him, to his own home in Ashfordly."

"It's his birthday today, Kate, he was supposed to be taking the day off. He'd fixed up a trip to Haworth, a visit to the Parsonage with the local Bronte Society."

"Oh, how terrible. He didn't mention that to me, Nick, but I can't imagine him wanting to leave home today."

"I need to speak to Graham, so I reckon I might find him at Ashfordly. Well, I mustn't delay you, and I must get myself down to Ashfordly. 'Bye."

She came across and kissed him. "Give Sergeant Blaketon and Graham my sympathies," she asked.

"Sure, love," and they left the washing up until the first one returned home.

As Nick approached Ashfordly Police Station on his motorcycle, a woman waved him down. She was carrying a bunch of flowers and as Nick halted to listen, she said, "Can you take these to the sergeant, Constable? For his wife, we are all so very sorry about what happened. These are from my family, all of us."

"Yes, of course, that is very kind of you, Mrs . . . er . . ."

"Just a friend, Constable, just a resident of Ashfordly who appreciates what the sergeant has done for us over the years."

"You're very kind," and Nick placed the flowers on his petrol tank as he covered the final yards. As he walked into the office bearing them, he saw that the table inside was smothered with more bunches, all shapes and sizes. Phil Bellamy was busy searching some index cards while Alf Ventress, enveloped within a cloud of smoke, was sitting before the floral covering of the table.

"A lady out there asked me to give these to serge," he said.

"Put 'em with the others, Nick," said Alf. "It's nice to know that somebody out there cares, eh?"

"Where is he?" asked Nick.

"He's gone out, Nick. He's cancelled his day off, he said he couldn't bear people being sorry for him during the Bronte outing, so he said he'd rather work. He went off in the car somewhere, but didn't say where. He is in uniform, by the way. Now that's unusual, not saying where he was going. Generally he insists on telling us his exact movements, but not this morning."

"But he was bearing up, you think?"

"Yes, very much so. There was no outward sign of grieving, Nick, they were divorced, remember."

"He still thought the world of her, Alf. In fact, I'd say he loved her. Anyway, it's young Graham I want to see. I need a statement from him before I can start putting my accident report together."

"You've missed him as well, Nick. He's taking Mrs Myers into hospital to see Denis, he's borrowed Blaketon's private car."

"Well, there's not much I can do until I've seen Graham; the report on the roadworthiness of the vehicles will take a few days to come through."

"And I've informed the coroner, Nick, he does want a post mortem, he suggested Monday. I've had words with the pathologist at Middlesbrough General and he can operate on Mrs Forrester at three o'clock, Monday. You'll have to go, being the officer who's dealing with the fatality."

"Right, I'll see to that. Now, any more broken offertory boxes this morning?"

"Not so far, Nick, but the churches are all full this morning. I can't see chummy raiding a church when it's full of worshippers."

"But today's when most of the cash is put into the boxes," Nick pointed out. "I'll bet chummy realises that, and once the congregations have gone home for their Yorkshire puddings and roast beef, he'll be out and about. We had about six done last Sunday afternoon, remember?"

"Don't remind me! That woman inspector's been ringing about that, telling us to get out and check all churches."

"Right, well, I'll visit a few on my patch between now and catching up with young Blaketon. Now, did serge get the present we left for him?"

"No, not yet. He didn't go into his office this morning," said Ventress. "He came in here from his car and said he was going straight out, so he didn't see what we'd bought him."

"It was a pair of hand carved book ends," said Phil. "For his collection of books."

"A nice choice," smiled Nick. "So, he'll get them later today. Do you think we should move them? Give him them on another day?"

"No," said Alf. "No, I think he'd appreciate our thoughts just now. Leave them until he finds them. Now, Phil, you'll need a bit of cash from us all. How much?"

"Thirty bob from each of you will cover it," said Phil.

"Right," and as Nick delved into his pocket for a £1 note and a ten-shilling note for Phil, he suddenly asked, "And Phil, what was the final score yesterday?"

"A draw," he said. "One all. The replay's on Wednesday, but I can't see Blaketon giving me time off for that. I'm supposed to be on lates."

"You did your bit for Whitby," smiled Nick. "Well, I'm off to visit a few churches, seeing it's Sunday. Tell Graham Blaketon I've been chasing him, Alf, it is important. Try to get him to agree to a time and place for a meeting."

"Right you are, Nick," said Alf, lighting another cigarette.

* * *

It was the sound of repeated peals of church bells that had caused Sergeant Blaketon to leave the police station in a somewhat sudden and unexplained manner. He was not a church-going man but that Sunday morning, with the trauma of finding Joan so badly injured and then having to cope with her death, he had been overcome by a sense of the power of God, and of the need to be alone with his thoughts.

He had decided to go to church. He had no wish to be part of a formalised service, he did not want the vicar of Ashfordly or any members of the well-meaning congregation to extend their sympathies to him. If they did, he felt he might be overcome with grief and unable to control his emotions.

For a senior policeman in uniform to be seen crying was not, he felt, the image that should be cultivated. He therefore decided to visit a church that was away from the town, a village church somewhere on the moors where the morning Sunday service was ended. He needed to be alone, to be in a place of solitude with his thoughts, to come to terms with the death of his wife, or to be precise, his ex-wife, as he had to keep reminding himself A peaceful church was ideal, he realised, and he could always explain his presence there by saying he was checking for signs of the offertory box thief. Not that he should have to explain himself, but he was always aware of the likelihood that someone he knew might arrive and be puzzled by his presence.

With his mind made up, Oscar Blaketon drove out of Ashfordly and made for the loftier heights of the North York Moors. He drove into the deep dales and then high onto the moors and eventually decided to visit Shelvingby. This was a remote hamlet high on a plateau on the edge of the hill.

Behind was the awesome and forbidding bulk of the moors, a terrible place in winter, and yet in summer the village was a place of serene beauty. A stream trickled from the heather, rippling over rocks and through gorges before easing to a gentler flow on the floor of the dale below Shelvingby. It was to the twelfth-century parish church of Shelvingby that Blaketon made his way. It was positioned almost half a mile from the edge of the village, on a flat portion of ground beside the stream.

He parked his car away from the church, in an old barn down a quiet lane so that it was concealed and then walked towards the Norman doorway. He passed the churchyard en route, peering at the tumble of gravestones over the dry-stone wall and thinking that some needed attention. Some of the graves, he noted, were well kept, but others were smothered in long grass and weeds. Such a pity, he felt. He went in through the oak lychgate and pinned into a glass fronted frame just inside the gate, was a notice which said that the service on Sunday morning was 9 a.m. Now it was nearly twelve noon and there was no sign of activity in or near the church. Experiencing a mixture of guilt and embarrassment should anyone see him, he made his way towards the porch.

He lifted the sneck on the huge studded oak door and it echoed inside the building, and so, leaving the door slightly ajar, he entered. As a mark of respect, he removed his cap and carried it. Inside, the light filtered through the beautiful colours of stained-glass windows, and there was an air of dampness about the building. Centuries of decay had attacked some of the woodwork and stonework, but the church was still standing on this riverside site as it had for some 700 years. He padded down the aisle, noting the kneelers, the prayer books resting on shelves in the pews, a candle burning near the altar and the brass lectern with its massive eagle motif. He stood for a few moments, somewhat in awe of the mystical presence which enveloped him, and then he noticed a small side chapel.

A Lady Chapel. It was a relic of Catholicism when it would have been dedicated to the Virgin Mary. Now the church was Protestant with the visible trappings of the old faith tom out and discarded. The chapel was dark, lit only by one small window in the high wall and there were no candles here.

He went across to the Lady Chapel and selected one of the empty pews, then knelt upon a kneeler which was already in position on the floor. Placing his cap on the pew at his side, Oscar Blaketon bowed his head, found a prayer book in the pew and opened it. Selecting a page at random, he found he had opened it at a prayer for the dead and so began to pray. But it was too much. He started to weep as his emotions overcame him in this place of peace.

CHAPTER XV

One of the outposts of Nick's beat was the village of Shelvingby. It was a small and remote community on the edge of the moors; it boasted a village inn which was popular with shooting parties and hikers, it had some splendid views, a street of sturdy stone cottages, a disused Methodist chapel and, in the valley below, the beautiful old parish church. There was not even a shop or a post office; there was no resident vicar either, the church being one of several served by the vicar of Slemmington. The villagers never created problems for Nick, they were a very law-abiding community. His only regular visits were for his quarterly checks of the stock records of local farmers and a bi-weekly visit to the pub around closing time. Most of his other visits were occasioned by minor traffic accidents involving visitors to the moors or ramblers who managed to lose themselves upon the surrounding hills.

It followed that the church was rarely visited by Nick and it was this lack of regular supervision that prompted him to turn towards Shelvingby that Sunday morning. On several occasions after the spate of thefts had started, he'd visited other churches closer to Aidensfield but Shelvingby, due to its remoteness, had not received similar attention. Possibly for the same reason, it had never suffered a raid.

That did mean, Nick considered, that it might be on the thief's shopping list and as Nick motored along the beautiful lanes, he felt he must check that lonely old church this morning. From his local knowledge, Nick knew that the service started at 9 a.m. and ended around 10 a.m. and that did suggest the giving of Sunday morning offerings. These would be placed in the offertory box, easy money for a visiting thief.

The ride from Aidensfield to Shelvingby comprises a series of steep hills on narrow lanes, a winding, undulating route which offers spectacular views across Rannockdale to the north and Craydale to the south. When Nick arrived in the village, mindful that the thief might be in residence, he decided to conceal his motorcycle. He left it on the outskirts, behind an old stone barn in a quiet field, and walked towards the church via a path across the fields. There was a brisk breeze this morning and he soon found himself enjoying the bracing moorland air. It brought a glow to his cheeks and he found himself thoroughly enjoying the stroll.

As he approached the church, however, he was aware of a vehicle parked among conifers about a hundred yards from the churchyard. The conifers were growing on common land, he knew, and there was a narrow green lane leading to them; Nick decided to inspect the vehicle which looked like an old pickup truck. When walking along the road, Nick noted, the truck was out of sight, perfectly concealed behind the trees, and it was sheer luck he had seen it. It could only be seen from the fields.

Policemen did need a piece of good fortune from time to time, and he wondered whether providence, or even God, was looking down upon him this Sunday morning. Was this the thief — had reports of visiting motorcycles been misleading? Nick's heart began to thump as he crept along the lane, hoping to surprise a possible thief. But the pickup belonged to Claude Jeremiah Greengrass! Nick could recognise that battered old truck anywhere!

So what was Claude doing here? Poaching? Then Nick remembered Claude's grass-mowing enterprise and wondered if the scruffy old character was working in Shelvingby church-yard this morning. He was not in the pickup, that was sure. Nick prowled around the vehicle, peering into the rear section and into the cab, but there was no Claude, no Alfred and no sign of any ill-gotten gains.

Leaving the vehicle, Nick walked through the small copse of sheltering trees and emerged at the other end with the church in full view. And there, swishing his scythe among the yews at the furthest end of the churchyard, was Claude Jeremiah Greengrass. Nick decided not to reveal his own presence, not at this stage, just in case Claude was in league with the offertory box thief. Although Nick did not readily suspect Claude of being responsible for these despicable thefts, the old rascal might be a look-out man, using his mowing chores as some kind of cover for a share of the proceeds? And so Nick crept away, not revealing his presence to Claude.

He made a quick search of the lanes near the church but failed to find any other vehicle nearby, so Nick then made his way to the porch. He was surprised to find the church door standing open just a fraction. He knew these old church door snecks made a loud rattling noise whenever the door was opened, so was the thief here? Working inside perhaps?

Nick crept in. He eased the heavy door open very very gently, making not a sound, and he stepped inside, easing the door to its former position. So far, he had not made a sound. The gloom was considerable; in fact, it was extremely dark inside and he had to stand silently for a few moments so that his eyes could adjust to the changed light. Standing in the shadows behind the door, he surveyed the interior of the musty old church, noting the columns, the altar and pulpit, the side chapel to his right and the base of the tower to his left. There seemed to be no one here, and yet that door had been ajar.

On silent soles, Nick went over to the area near the front and saw the offertory box fixed to a wooden panel on the wall. It was wooden too, but it was intact. He tried to lift the lid but it was firm; it was secured by a stout padlock so had he disturbed the thief? The fellow could be hiding here, there were plenty of dark corners, including places like the vestry and even the bell tower itself. Nick knew he'd have to search the entire church. But if the thief was hiding, then he must know Nick was here!

He could be concealed and he would be armed with the instrument he was using to smash open the boxes. Nick knew he must take great care during the next few minutes. Removing his helmet out of respect for the house of God, Nick started by creeping along the wall from the door, heading towards the Lady Chapel. His soft soled boots were noiseless and as he reached the chapel from the rear, he saw a dark figure kneeling in one of the pews, head bowed as if in prayer.

Nick halted. It looked like the vicar. Nick felt he was intruding now. The presence of this person did account for the partially open door, but, as Nick took stock of the situation, it did occur to him that this could indeed be the thief, pretending to be a man of prayer! Nick needed to take a closer look. He moved a yard or so further along the stone floor, his presence not making the tiniest of noises and then he had a shock. He saw the chevrons of the sleeves of the dark coat, he saw the police cap lying on the pew, he saw the familiar grey hair and ears of Sergeant Blaketon! So this is where he was!

Nick decided not to interrupt Sergeant Blaketon in his grief. Clearly, the fellow had been seeking some remote and secluded place to kneel in prayer, somewhere to remember Joan. Perhaps this was one of their favourite places? A walk in the dale and a visit to the church for quiet moments together? Nick knew he must never intrude and so, leaving Blaketon with his head in his hands, either in tears or in prayer, Nick retreated.

He moved away from the chapel, edging back towards the door while wondering how he was going to search the rest of the church without disturbing Sergeant Blaketon. He regained the entrance without any problems; the door was still open just a fraction and it was at that moment, that Nick heard the faint sound of a motorcycle. The noise filtered through the open door. It was a small machine by the sound of it but it stopped somewhere out of sight. Nick peered through the crack but saw nothing. Whoever it was had parked a short distance from the main entrance.

Nick's heart began to beat now; this time, it might be the thief . . . quickly, he moved away from the door and concealed himself in the darkness behind a pillar at the rear. From here, he could see the door and the offertory box.

Nick settled down to wait.

* * *

For Claude Jeremiah Greengrass, it seemed as if his urgent mission was never going to be accomplished. He had trudged around almost every churchyard in, around and upon the North York Moors without even a hint of success. He had chopped down acres of long grass, mown countless crops of nettles and hacked his way through briars, hawthorn shrubs and bottery bushes. He had rediscovered lost graves, tidied neglected graves, struggled with the inscriptions on ancient graves and even found the graves of some long forgotten Greengrass ancestors, such as great great great uncle Jeremiah.

But he had not found what he sought.

On that Sunday morning, therefore, disillusioned by his lack of success, he was on the point of ending his quest. His feet were sore, his legs were tired and his scythe was blunt through striking many marble gravestones and lots of concealed and broken flower pots and it was well past opening time at the Aidensfield Arms. Day after day he had slogged away with his scythe, trudging among thousands of graves while plodding what seemed hundreds of miles with his blisters and aching limbs. And for what? Nothing.

At Shelvingby that Sunday morning, therefore, he decided that if he did not succeed today, he would cease his mission. He'd had enough and besides, Alfred was getting bored. The shaggy mongrel had chased rabbits, dug holes, barked at mourners and cocked his leg against fresh pots of flowers while his lord and master had been studying ancient inscriptions upon hundreds upon hundreds of graves.

Claude sat down on a flat-topped grave for a rest. Alfred came to his side and nuzzled his head against Claude's leg; Claude rubbed his ears and stroked his faithful dog.

"He's got to be somewhere, Alfred," he spoke softly to the dog. "That man's got to be buried somewhere . . . if we've looked at one grave near Aidensfield, we've looked at dozens."

Alfred whined in sympathy as Claude pulled the tattered piece of newspaper from his coat pocket. He read it again, just to be sure he was on the right track.

The short feature told how an American industrialist called Jasper J. Perryhawk had recently discovered his English roots. His ancestors came from a village near Aidensfield in the North York Moors having lived in and around the moors for generations. It seems that in 1778, a Silas Perryhawk, along with his wife and seven children, had emigrated to America from Aidensfield. There he had settled to found a new family in the United States, and the present Jasper J. was a direct descendant. The last of the English Perryhawks, however, was Linus Otto Perryhawk. Father of Silas, he had died on 4th July 1776, the very day of the Declaration of Independence for the United States of America.

Jasper J., now rich and successful, wanted to relocate the grave of Linus Otto. Jasper was himself not very fit now, being 82 years old, and it was his life's ambition to find that grave before he died. He had searched his own family tree from the sources he had amassed in the USA, but had produced no success. He was too frail to travel to England, and so an American news agency had sent the story to the British newspapers in the hope that someone might read of the old man's quest and even find the grave and inform old Mr Perryhawk.

Mr Perryhawk had lodged £150 with an English solicitor and that money was awaiting the person who located the grave and then provided proof of both its existence and whereabouts to the solicitor. The solicitor's name and address were given — he lived and worked in Ashfordly.

And so Claude had set out upon that mission, thinking it was an easy way to earn £150. After all, a man's average wage was about £850 a year, so £150 was a very useful sum.

Claude had not told anyone of his quest. If he let anybody else know about this, they might find the grave. And so he'd tom out the newspaper cutting and had set out to find the grave of the long-lost Perryhawk, pretending to be cutting grass and tidying churchyards. But so far, he'd found nothing, although he had chopped down a lot of long grass.

Alfred was whining now, anxious to be off, his big dark eyes looking into those of his master.

"You're a slave driver, Alfred Greengrass," said Claude struggling to his feet. "By, I don't know, there's no rest for the wicked . . . if you pardon the expression," and Claude raised his eyes as if to heaven. "Come on, Alfred, it's time to go. We've finished now."

The moment Claude began to move, Alfred recognised the signs and dashed off, barking and chasing among the tombstones, flushing out sparrows and robins, frightening a family of rabbits and making some shrews squeak in alarm. He was a very happy dog.

"Alfred, show some respect!" bellowed Claude. "Remember where you are . . . Alfred!"

Claude's shout of horror arose because Alfred had stopped at an old tombstone, one leaning over and caked with the lichens of centuries past.

Alfred had cocked his leg and was directing a hot stream at the edge of the tombstone, a look of absolute pleasure and relief on his bewhiskered features.

"Alfred, lay off! That's hallowed ground, you can't go around doing that sort of thing here . . . Alfred!" and Claude began to shamble across to the dog.

But Alfred's joy was such that he ignored Claude, at least for the duration of his achievement. By the time he had ended his moment of bliss, Claude had arrived and stooped down to brush the dog away from the grave. And then he saw the inscription.

At the top of the stone were the initials RIP, and then it said, "Sacred to the memory of Linus Otto Perryhawk, late of Aidensfield and a stalwart of this parish, who departed this life 4th July 1776 aged 46 years."

Beneath was added the words,

Beneath lie mouldering into dust,
A carpenter's remains;
A man laborious, honest, just;
His character sustains.

"Alfred, I could kiss you," cried Claude. "This is him! We're rich. And it's opening time in Aidensfield, time to celebrate I reckon. Hang on, I'll have to write all this down . . . now, where's my pencil . . . and notebook . . ."

Claude searched his pockets for the pencil and notebook he had brought especially for this job and had just completed his copying of the inscription when he heard the distinctive sounds of a small motorcycle. It was approaching the church gates but then it halted some distance away. Claude, mindful of Constable Rowan's inquisition about offertory box thefts, ducked down behind the gravestone, calling Alfred to his side with a low owl-like whistle.

Alfred, trained to be silent at this poacher's command, obeyed instantly. And so man and dog waited behind the tombstone. Claude recalled that motorcycle noises had been heard in the vicinity of earlier thefts as his khaki overcoat merged with the lush vegetation at this distant end of the graveyard. And then he saw a young man heading for the gate. He was walking from the far side of the church, having left his machine round the back. At this point, he was too far away for Claude to see who it was, but the youth marched quickly along the path towards the porch, looked around himself for signs of other people, and then boldly walked into the church.

CHAPTER XVI

Waiting in the gloom, Nick's heart began to pound as he heard footsteps approaching. Through the narrow gap between the door and the doorpost, he saw shadowy movements and then the door was eased open very slowly and very quietly. Nick remained in the shadows, his dark uniform almost invisible and he moved behind the sheltering pillar. Blaketon was still in the side chapel, apparently oblivious to Nick's presence and similarly oblivious to the approach of the newcomer.

The door was pushed wider and a head appeared; Nick couldn't be sure who it was at this stage, the light behind the incomer making him appear as a silhouette, but it was a man, and he was entering the church in a very stealthy manner. Suddenly, he was moving faster. Once he was inside, he left the door standing open, probably to facilitate a swift escape if indeed he was the thief, and then moved quickly across the floor of the church towards the offertory box.

Nick now realised that this was indeed the thief he was seeking. The man, head down and dressed in a dark anorak, pulled a large screwdriver from the inside of his anorak and then tested the lid of the offertory box. It was closed and locked. Even though the fellow's intentions seemed to be very clear, Nick knew he must wait until the right moment.

He must catch this man in the act of actually breaking open the box because he must obtain evidence of his criminal intent. If Nick did not wait until that moment, a court might dismiss any charge against the felon. To catch the fellow merely in possession of a screwdriver as he approached the box was not enough to satisfy some courts. The fellow could say he was a woodworker and was going to put some cash into the box . . . after all, anyone could be carrying a screwdriver and possession of a screwdriver wasn't illegal. So Nick had to wait until the fellow was actually breaking into the box. There would be some damage but it was a small price to pay for the arrest and conviction of a persistent thief.

Peering around the pillar, Nick saw the man look towards the altar; Blaketon was out of sight from that point and Nick knew that the sergeant would be deep in concentration, so much so that he was blissfully unaware of anyone else at that moment. Then Nick saw the blade of the large screwdriver; it flashed momentarily in the light from the open door as it was inserted between the lid and the side of the offertory box. There was a crunching of wood as the man exerted pressure upon the screwdriver by leaning his weight upon it and it was at that instant that Nick moved towards him.

On silent soles, he crossed the stone floor of the church, creeping up to the thief from the rear and still not recognising the man. As the box lid was levered off with a crisp sound of breaking wood, Nick seized him from behind.

At the same time, he hissed, "Police. Stay right where you are, don't move an inch! You're under arrest."

The man, shocked and surprised by the sudden turn of events and the arms which immobilised him from behind, produced a loud cry of alarm and suddenly flopped to the floor, taking Nick by surprise. Nick was forced to release his hold.

Now the man was escaping. He threw the screwdriver to the floor with a loud clatter as Nick leapt forward again, this time grabbing an arm as the man was heading for the open doorway. Nick held on, he managed to trip the man with a well-aimed kick at his ankles and as he stumbled, Nick saw that it was Gordon Turnbull.

"Gordon, you! Of all the people . . ."

But Turnbull was fighting like a wild cat, arms and legs flailing as Nick struggled to detain him. But Turnbull was now immobilised, even if he was thrashing wildly. Nick had him in a very effective arm lock.

"It's no good, Gordon, I recognise you . . . stop struggling," and at that moment, Nick heard the familiar voice of Sergeant Blaketon saying, "Nice one, Rowan. Caught in the act, eh? That's how we like it," and he stooped to the floor to pick up the fallen screwdriver. "And we've got some real evidence, eh? I reckon this screwdriver's blade will match the plaster casts of the marks we've found on other offertory boxes, don't you, Rowan?"

"I'm sure you're right, Sergeant," smiled Nick, looking at Blaketon. He had his cap on, his face was its usual stem self and there was no sign of his grief. Blaketon was back at work, back at being a policeman.

Held in the arm lock with his head and back bowed beneath the pressure, Gordon Turnbull was weeping.

"Look, I'm sorry . . . I really am, Mr Rowan, I'll repay everything, I'll repair any damage . . ."

"You can tell that to the court and to the church authorities, Gordon," said Nick quietly. "Now, it's handcuffs time."

With Blaketon standing before the dejected Gordon, Nick pulled a pair of handcuffs from his pocket and slipped them upon Gordon's wrists, locking them securely before Gordon's stomach. The young man now looked defeated and deflated, a picture of misery and regret.

"I'm sorry, I really am . . . I don't know why I did it . . ."

"Money, perhaps?" said Nick. "Greed, maybe? Trying to keep up a lifestyle to impress your friends? I wonder what they'll think of you now, Gordon?"

"Take him to my car, Rowan," said Sergeant Blaketon. "It's in a barn near Ashberry Farm, nicely concealed."

Then Blaketon turned to Gordon Turnbull and said, "It's Ashfordly Police Station for you, young man, and then an appearance at the magistrate's court. So, I suggest you start thinking hard about what you've done."

The lad made no reply as Sergeant Blaketon continued, "We would appreciate a list of all the other churches you've raided and then the court can take all those cases into consideration. It'll wipe the slate clean at one go, a tough lesson, but all of your own making. All right, Rowan, off we go. We'll come back for your bike when we've dealt with this young thief."

Marching Gordon before him, Nick left the church as Sergeant Blaketon accompanied him and as they emerged into the bright sunlight of that Sunday, the first person they saw was Claude Jeremiah Greengrass. Accompanied by the faithful Alfred, he was carrying a scythe and a strickle, and had a happy smile on his face. At exactly the moment that Nick saw Claude, Claude saw Nick and Blaketon. His smile of triumph and happiness vanished in a trice.

"What the . . ." snapped Claude. "Are you lot spying on me? Can't a chap go about his lawful business on a good Sunday without half the county constabulary trailing him?"

"So what are you doing here, Greengrass?" bellowed Sergeant Blaketon.

"Minding my own business," retorted Claude. "Doing my service to the community, cutting grass, aren't I?" and then he realised that Gordon was being marched between the officers with his hands in cuffs. "Hello, so what's Gordon been doing?"

"Raiding offertory boxes, Greengrass," said Sergeant Blaketon. "Only we were waiting for him this time. So what are you doing here? His look-out perhaps? A double act, was it? Greengrass keeping a vigil for the police while Gordon breaks into the boxes, each taking a share of the proceeds. Sounds perfectly reasonable to me."

"No, Mr Blaketon," whispered Gordon. "Claude's nothing to do with this, I'm on my own."

"So what *are* you doing here, Claude?" Nick asked his old adversary.

"Making money, aren't I?" beamed Claude.

"You told me you weren't charging the vicars for cutting their grass?" Nick said, holding onto Gordon's arm.

"I wasn't. It's all free is that — part of my community service," grinned Claude. "I've tidied hundreds of neglected graves, I have, and found some Greengrass ancestors."

"So the money-making, Claude?" persisted Nick. "How come you've made money out of all this?"

"Well, I can tell you now because my Alfred has made a big discovery today, you see, here in his churchyard," smiled Claude. "This rich Yank is seeking his roots, see, and can't get over the pond to visit all our churchyards to find his ancestors. So he advertised for help, he's put money into a solicitor's office, the cash is waiting for the chap who finds the grave. Well, it's here, I've found it. Linus Otto Perryhawk no less, famous in America, I'll bet."

"Really?" smiled Nick. "You've made yourself an honest bit of money, eh?"

"Aye, I have that. And he might even give me a free trip to New York to see the sights, eh? So I'm in the money, and it's all legal."

"All right, Claude," grinned Nick. "I believe you, many wouldn't."

"Well, it does show a bit of enterprise, and perhaps will show this young thief there are ways of earning money without stealing from churches and charities. Come along, Rowan, it's time to deal with this thief. The inspector will be pleased."

Claude watched them march Gordon towards the gate and then said, "Gordon, you ought to be ashamed of yourself! I'm no angel, but I'd never rob a church."

And Gordon hung his head low as he was taken to the waiting police car.

At Ashfordly Police Station, Gordon was searched and then placed in the cell while Nick checked the list of offertory box thefts which had occurred in recent months. He made a list of every one, with its location and the amount estimated to have been stolen, together with the MO of the crimes. In all cases, wooden boxes had been attacked with a screwdriver bearing a three-eighths of an inch blade. And when all these were presented to Gordon Turnbull, he readily admitted each one and this was incorporated in a lengthy statement of confession.

He also admitted stealing cash from some shops he had entered quite legitimately, sneaking his hand into the tills while the assistant's attention was elsewhere. He had no idea of the precise amount he had stolen over the past two years, but it came to several hundred pounds. And it was all to finance his desire for smart cars and pretty girls.

While Nick was dealing with the arrest and charging procedures, Sergeant Blaketon went into his office. His first shock was the volume of flowers lying around the walls and floor, then the birthday present and cards on his desk and finally the handwritten greeting stuck high on the wall. For a moment, tears came into his eyes; he had no idea that the public thought so highly of him, and as he opened his present, he was touched by the gift of book ends from the men at his station. He went back into the enquiry office where Alf Ventress was manning the phone while Nick entered Turnbull's details on the charge sheet.

"Er, Ventress, Rowan, I don't quite know how to put this, but, well, I'd like to thank you for your kindness, the present, book ends . . . and all those flowers from the townspeople . . . it really does restore one's faith in human nature . . ." and then, his eyes brimming with tears, he hurried back into his office saying, "And it's made my birthday a little happier by being able to ring that woman to say we've caught the offertory box thief!"

In his office, calmer now but with moisture glistening on his cheeks, Sergeant Blaketon picked up the telephone and dialled Whitby Police Station, asking for Inspector Murchison.

"It's Blaketon, ma'am," he announced himself.

"Look, Sergeant, I'm terribly sorry about the loss of Mrs Forrester . . . I had no idea, I mean, yesterday, when I despatched you to the scene. Had I known, I would have ordered some other officer to attend."

"That is quite all right, ma'am," he said stiffly. "I have my duty to do without fear or favour, and I have some very good officers here to help me. They were in control."

"Yes, well, I do extend my deepest sympathy to you."

"Thank you, now I have some better news," and he told her about the arrest of Gordon Turnbull and his admission of a string of other crimes. Inspector Murchison expressed her appreciation of that work and said that the officers of Ashfordly section had done some very good work this weekend. Work of the highest calibre.

"They are very sound officers, ma'am," said Blaketon with some pride. "Even if they do watch football matches through holes in the fence when they're supposed to be on car parking duties!"

"I'm beginning to realise that," she had to admit. "Now, Sergeant, there is the question of the inquest on Mrs Forrester and the possibility of a prosecution of the other person involved in the fatality, Denis Myers. Clearly, the file will take some time to prepare bearing in mind the delay in obtaining the reports on vehicle examinations and any medical evidence that is required. I am wondering, in view of the circumstances, whether you feel it would be better for another officer to prepare the fatal accident file. Perhaps one from outside Ashfordly section?"

"The moment I realised my ex-wife was the casualty," said Blaketon, "I placed the responsibility for dealing with the incident in the hands of PC Rowan, ma'am. He is a young officer but he is very capable and I have no qualms about leaving him in control. I know he will compile a full and comprehensive report about the accident, and he will be totally impartial in his assessment of any responsibility."

"I admire your confidence in your men, Sergeant. All right, I'll leave it with Rowan. Now, how about taking the rest of today off, Sergeant? No one would expect you to be working today."

"I'd rather be at work, ma'am, than moping around in my house all alone. I am in very good company here, my men are showing a lot of compassion and support, so I don't want to be anywhere else. But thank you for your thoughts."

And so Oscar Blaketon took a deep breath and went back to speak with Rowan and Ventress.

"Serge," Nick spoke quietly. "On the subject of the accident, I still need to speak to Graham. I believe he stayed the night at your house?"

"He did, but he took my private car this morning and drove Mrs Myers into Whitby to visit Denis in hospital. He's not back yet."

"Maybe, when he does get back, you'd let me know?"

"He didn't see anything, Rowan, he told you that in the hospital."

"I'd still like to take a statement from him, Sergeant," insisted Nick.

"As you wish, Rowan," said Sergeant Blaketon. "Now, how are things progressing with the offertory box thief?"

"I'm ready to charge him with that attempted theft at Shelvingby, Sergeant, and with all the others he has admitted. I've prepared the charge sheet. It's ready for your signature."

"Good, well, bring him from the cell. I'll charge him and then we'll bail him out to appear at court next Saturday." And so the work of Ashfordly Police Station was getting back to normal.

CHAPTER XVII

By Sunday evening, both Nick and Kate were exhausted. The combination of the overnight duties last night coupled with an early start that morning and the emotional pressures of dealing with the loss of someone so close to them had mentally and physically drained both. Neither had any wish to go out for a dinner. Instead, they had helped one another to make a meal which they would eat from trays before the blazing fire at Aidensfield Police House. Both were now off duty and so they had changed into something casual, each vowing not to answer the telephone if it rang. This evening was for them, to be alone and to relax.

Their enjoyment of the meal was leisurely and wholesome and after washing the pots, they settled down to read. Both liked reading; Kate enjoyed a whole range of classic novels, ranging from Dickens to Thomas Hardy while Nick preferred nonfiction — he was studying the history of the British motor car. As they read, they had a glass of wine; as the relaxing evening moved on, each began to feel tired and ready for bed.

"I think I'll turn in," Kate announced. "I know it's still early but I'm shattered, Nick."

"Me too, but you know what'll happen if we both turn in — the phone will ring or somebody will come knocking on the door! And you're still worrying about Denis, aren't you?"

"Yes, I am," she admitted. "It was a terrible thing to say, Nick, about me not warning him about the effect of those tablets, especially when it's not true. It makes me look as if I'm not doing my job properly. Did you ask Graham Blaketon if he knew about Denis' tablets?"

"I haven't managed to track him down yet," he admitted. "He spent the night with his father, at Ashfordly, then used Blaketon's private car to take Mrs Myers to see Denis."

"Poor Graham, he'll be without a home now, won't he? Do you think he'll move in with his father?"

Nick shrugged. "They've never really got on in the past, but Graham is a bit more mature now. It might just work and I'm sure Blaketon will offer the lad a home. It could be the finest thing for both of them, Blaketon does appreciate a home life, you know, even though he never seems to take time off."

"Graham will need a father's support just now," said Kate. "When I saw him at the hospital, he was in a very subdued mood. He was blaming himself for what happened."

"I can't see why," said Nick. "Mind, I don't know the full story yet, which is why I must interview him before too long. He wouldn't say a thing the last time I spoke to him, he just said he knew nothing and had seen nothing. But I think he does know something, especially the fact that those kids were racing along those lanes."

"You won't forget to ask him whether Denis knew the risks when taking those antihistamines?" she persisted.

"I'll ask him, I promise," Nick assured her. "Now, how about that early night?"

"Right, you make the cocoa and I'll warm the bed up!" she smiled, rising to her feet. And at that moment, there was a knock on the door.

"Oh, no," she groaned. "I knew it! It always happens! Don't answer it, Nick, please."

"I can't ignore it," he said. "It might be somebody in trouble, you never know . . ."

"Yes, of course. You're right," she conceded. "See who it is."

And when Nick opened the door, Graham Blaketon was standing there looking distraught and miserable, and his father was immediately behind him, stem faced and very much the police officer on duty. He was in his uniform.

"Rowan," he nodded a greeting.

"Sergeant Blaketon!" Nick sounded surprised. "This is a surprise."

Graham spoke next. "Dad says I should come and tell you all about the accident," he said quietly.

"You'd better come in," invited Nick and he opened the door wide to admit his guests. Instead of dealing with them in the office adjoining the house, he took them into the lounge.

"It's Sergeant Blaketon and Graham," Nick told Kate. "They've come about the accident. Tea, Sergeant? Coffee?"

"A cup of tea would be very welcome," said Sergeant Blaketon.

"Graham?" Nick tried to put the youth at his ease; quite clearly, he was distressed and upset about the predicament in which he found himself.

"Thanks, yes, tea would be fine."

"I'll make the tea," offered Kate. As she went into the kitchen to brew the tea, Nick settled them before the fire, hoping they would both relax and that they would feel more comfortable here than in the clinical atmosphere of the hospital, still fresh in their memories.

"Graham wants to say something to you," began Blaketon looking decidedly uncomfortable.

Nick, standing before the fire, looked down at the unhappy youth, then changed his stance and settled in an armchair next to Graham. Now both were on a level and Nick smiled.

"So, Graham, what do you wish to say?"

Graham took a deep breath, saying, "Dad says I should tell the truth, about everything," he began. "You know,

Denis driving his dad's car without being accompanied by a passed driver, being a learner, and the Killing Pits Club doing those trials around the village and all that."

"All right," said Nick. "Now, I'm sure your father will have explained that I must take it all down in writing, for my accident report that is. So what I want you to do first is to tell me everything, and then we'll put it all on paper."

With gentle questioning by Nick, particularly about the chronology of events, Graham told his version of things. He told Nick about the Killing Pits Club and how they raced around the moors, the slowest having to pay for the drinks after the trials, and how Denis could never become a club member because he had no car of his own. And he couldn't drive either, not alone, because he hadn't passed his driving test. Graham went on to explain how Mrs Myers had allowed them to take the family car, trusting Graham to look after it, but yesterday afternoon, when the club was short of members, Graham had been asked to serve as the half-way marshal. Graham explained that his half-way position was at Bracken Corner, a notoriously bad corner with steep downward hills dropping into it from either direction. He had to time all the cars as they passed through, and also ensure none took a short cut.

Unknown to him, Gordon Turnbull had tempted Denis into attempting a fast run in his father's car, persuading him to remove his "L" plates and Denis, so anxious to do well and so keen to become a member of the Killing Pits Club, had agreed.

At this point, Kate came in with mugs of hot tea for them all, and some biscuits.

Nick paused in his questioning as Kate distributed the refreshments, and then, when she was seated in her chair, Nick resumed.

"Graham," Nick asked. "Was Denis fit to drive?"

"He was just a learner," Graham said.

"No, I don't mean that," Nick pressed him. "I mean was he ill? You see he'd been to visit the doctor and she'd given him some tablets."

"He had a rash, I saw it on his arms when he went to bed. I shared a room with him."

"And was he taking pills for the rash?" continued Nick.

"Yes, I can't remember their name, but he was taking them in the morning, one at dinner time and another before he went to sleep. I saw him taking them and when he showed me the rash, I asked if it was catching. He said it wasn't. He said he hadn't to drive while taking the tablets or have a drink of beer, they would make him dizzy. The doctor had told him not to drive, so he told me, so he was off work as well, for a week."

"Thank you," breathed Kate. "So I did warn him!"

"Warn him?" asked Blaketon. "What about, might I ask?"

Kate smiled. "Denis had an allergy, Sergeant, I do not know what would have caused it, but I put him on a course of antihistamine tablets for a week. The allergy had caused a nasty rash on his arms and other parts of the body, and it would be uncomfortable. However, the tablets do make the patient feel dizzy at times, and so I warned Denis of the dangers of becoming dizzy while driving, or working on scaffolding and even after having alcohol. I made him promise not to drink or drive while on the course of tablets, and I signed him off work until he'd recovered."

"So those tablets would adversely affect his driving?"

"Yes, very much so. He'd get dizzy spells which would make him incapable of having full control of the vehicle, but Denis swears I never warned him of the consequences. Graham has just confirmed that I did warn him, Sergeant. Denis should never have been driving at all, not even his motorbike."

"Point taken," said Blaketon. "You'll incorporate that in Graham's statement, Rowan?"

"Of course, Sergeant. Now, Graham, this is the nasty bit for you, and for your father. From evidence collected at the scene at the time of the accident, and from tyre-marks we have recorded, it does seem that Mrs Blaketon, er Mrs Forrester, was driving on the wrong side of the road. You were there, Graham, so I need to know exactly what you saw."

Graham nodded.

"She only went to the wrong side at the last minute, Mr Rowan. She was driving perfectly normally just before the accident. I saw her coming down the hill, into the sharp bend, and at the same time saw Denis racing along, into the same sharp bend. I could see the two cars would meet there, I knew there'd be a collision."

"Denis was going too fast, was he?" asked Nick gently.

"Yes, far too fast. He didn't seem to be in full control, not like a normal driver would have been . . . I could see there was going to be an accident unless I stopped one of them. So I waved my arms at mum, I was standing high above the road really, and don't know whether she could see me, but I ran about and waved my arms, shouting for her to slow down or stop."

There were signs of distress in the lad's voice now, but Nick must not allow him to waver, not at this stage.

"Go on, Graham," he encouraged him.

"I know she saw me waving my arms about, she was very surprised to see me there, in the middle of the moor, and I think she must have thought I'd had an accident or some-thing . . . anyway, she swerved the minute she saw me . . . and that's when Denis ran into her. It was awful, Mr Rowan, really awful . . . I mean, I couldn't do anything . . . nothing . . . I ran down to help and then some other cars came."

"Thank you, Graham," breathed Nick. "You've been very brave and I appreciate it."

"It was my fault, Mr Rowan, it was all my fault! If I hadn't borrowed Denis' dad's car, if I hadn't waved at mum, if I hadn't agreed to be the half-way marshal, or told the club the police were all away at Whitby . . . well, this wouldn't have happened."

"Graham, you must never blame yourself, none of this was your fault. We will be speaking to Denis in due course, when he's fit to be interviewed, but you mustn't blame yourself." Sergeant Blaketon leaned across and patted his son on the arm.

"PC Rowan is right, Graham, you must not blame yourself."

"There are still some more terrible ordeals ahead for you, Graham," added Nick. "The inquest for one thing, and maybe a court appearance if we decide to charge Denis with anything."

"Dangerous driving, you mean?"

"It could be worse than that," Nick spoke solemnly. "Driving under the influence of drugs, perhaps, or even causing death by dangerous driving. I know he has been medically examined at the hospital, so we will have to see what the experts say about the amount of drugs in his system."

Graham was weeping now. Putting his head on his father's shoulder, he was sobbing quietly to himself as Sergeant Blaketon, in a rare touch of gentleness, put his arm about the lad and cradled him to his breast.

"Thank you for being so gentle with him, Rowan," said Blaketon. "It's so tough for him, thinking he's responsible for Joan's death."

"It was a most unfortunate accident, Sergeant," was all Nick could say. "I really am most sorry."

"If there is any fault, Graham," said Kate, "a lot will lie on Denis' shoulders. He might need help from you, Graham, to get over this. I know he's trying to talk himself out of any responsibility, but once the full realisation of his actions filters through to him, I think he might need your support."

"But he killed my mother . . ." sobbed Graham.

"An accident killed your mother," said Nick.

"We've got a lot of enquiries to complete and soul-searching to do before we start blaming people, Graham," said Sergeant Blaketon. "Come along, son, it's time we were going home."

And at that point, there was another knock on the door.

"Who on earth is this?" breathed Nick.

"I'll get it," offered Kate.

CHAPTER XVIII

When Kate opened the door, she found a crowd of young people standing there, many of whom she recognised as youths and girls from Aidensfield.

"Doctor Rowan?" a tall youth stepped forward. "I'm sorry to come at this time of night, but, well, we suddenly decided we should come and see PC Rowan."

"Oh, really, what about?" she asked.

"Well, all sorts," the lad seemed somewhat diffident about his purpose. "Mainly, though, about the awful accident, and the Killing Pits Club, and so on."

"Well, you'd better come in, all of you," and she held the door wide open so that they could crowd into the house. She led them into the lounge. Some eighteen or nineteen youngsters crowded into the police house and one of them, a girl, was carrying a paper carrier bag.

"Nick, there's someone to see you," smiled Kate. "In fact, a lot of someones to see you!"

Nick turned to see the influx of people and was momentarily shocked. He recognised the leading youth, a lad called Duncan Saunders.

"Hello, Duncan, what's this? A deputation?"

Duncan, rather nervous at seeing Sergeant Blaketon sitting in the room with his son, said, "Er, no, but we've had a meeting of the Killing Pits Club . . ."

"We'll leave, PC Rowan," said Blaketon, rising to his feet. "I think we have concluded our business."

"No, please, don't go, Sergeant," Duncan was sufficiently quick thinking to ask Blaketon and Graham to remain. "What I have to say does affect you as well, both of you."

"Oh, well, if you say so, I don't want to intrude on something private, you know."

"It's not private, Sergeant, and the first thing I'd, er, we'd all like to say, is how sorry we were about your ex-wife's death. It really shocked us, all of us. We are members of the Killing Pits Club, you see, and we all feel responsible . . ."

"It was an accident," grunted Blaketon. "I'm not one for apportioning blame without hearing all sides."

"Well," smiled Nick. "Is this all the club, then? Every member?"

"Except Gordon," said Duncan with just a hint of a wry smile. "We often wondered where he got his money from. He won't be allowed back in, Mr Rowan, not after what he's done."

"Well, I can't find chairs for you all, so you'd better sit on the floor or wherever you can find a space," and so they all settled down before Nick asked, "So why are you all here?"

"We had a club meeting tonight, Mr Rowan, at the Aidensfield Arms, and we decided that we should put the club on a proper footing. You know, with a chairman, and a committee and rules and things. We've been daft, really, but all we want is something to do with our time, and we all love cars so we wondered if you would be chairman. I mean, you have that lovely MG and you know about the law, and you could explain things to us, about the laws, about driving skills, about car maintenance and so on. That's what we'd like to do."

Nick looked at Sergeant Blaketon for guidance.

"It sounds a fine idea to me, Rowan," he smiled. "Youngsters do need guidance with their motoring and I'm sure you could do a good job."

"Right," said Nick. "If I am to be chairman, this is what I want from you all. I want a proper club, run with responsibility, with some of you elected as committee members. I'll be chairman, but I'll need a secretary and first of all, I would want to instigate the Joan Forrester Memorial Trophy for some event that the new committee will determine. And I want you all to attend her funeral, which is to be arranged soon — that is a mark of respect, the least you can do."

They sat around and listened in silence as Nick walked up and down, expressing his views. He told them about the need for car maintenance, for the need not to upset the villagers with noisy vehicles and for a new sense of responsibility to be created. They all agreed with him.

He spent about twenty minutes outlining his idea and then concluded by saying, "I think we should change the name too. Killing Pits Club sounds terrible!"

"What shall we call it?" asked Duncan.

"How about the Aidensfield and District Motoring Club?" suggested Nick. "And open it to all motorists, motorcyclists included, so that people like Denis can join and be welcomed. If you will agree to help me run the new club along sensible lines, then I will be pleased to act as chairman, at least for one term of office. OK?"

The expressions on their faces showed a mixture of relief and pleasure, and without exception they agreed to consider his ideas. He suggested another meeting next Friday night, at the Aidensfield Arms, when he would produce his suggestion for a set of club rules and some ideas for club outings and events.

When they had all digested his views, Duncan said, "Well, that's fine. We were so nervous about coming here, in view of what's happened."

Blaketon spoke now. "I think what you did took a lot of courage, from all of you. I am full of admiration and think the new club is a very worthwhile one. You have my full support."

"Maybe you should be President, Sergeant?" smiled Nick, and the assembled youngsters cheered spontaneously.

Blaketon beamed and said, "Yes, yes, I would like that. What a lovely idea."

And so they all clambered to their feet as they prepared to leave, but one of the girls, the one carrying the carrier bag, came forward.

"Mr Rowan," she said. "You know we all went to the scene of the accident yesterday, well, when everyone had left, I found this on the moor. I think it had been thrown out of one of the cars, I thought I'd better hand it in."

From her carrier bag she lifted a brown paper parcel bearing a gift tag, and handed it to Nick. He saw the hand-writing on the label: it said, "To Oscar, with love and wishing you a happy birthday, Joan and Graham."

Nick swallowed.

"It's for you, Sergeant," he said, passing the gift across to Sergeant Blaketon.

THE END

ALSO BY NICHOLAS RHEA

MORE COMING SOON

Gorgeous new Kindle editions of the **Constable Nick** books soon to be released by Joffe Books.

Don't miss a book in the series — join our mailing list:

www.joffebooks.com

FREE KINDLE BOOKS

Thank you for reading this book. If you enjoyed it please leave feedback on Amazon or Goodreads, and if there is anything we missed or you have a question about, then please get in touch. The author and publishing team appreciate your feedback and time reading this book.

We're very grateful to eagle-eyed readers who take the time to contact us. Please send any errors you find to corrections@joffebooks.com. We'll get them fixed ASAP.

Made in the USA
Las Vegas, NV
19 January 2021

16208594R00094